Last Boat to Cadiz

Also by Barnaby Conrad

Fiction

The Innocent Villa
Matador
Dangerfield
Zorro: A Fox in the City
Endangered (with Niels Mortensen)
Fire Below Zero (with Nico Mastorakis)
Keepers of the Secret (with Nico Mastorakis)

Translations

The Wounds of Hunger (Spota)
The Second Life of Captain Contreras (Luca de Tena)
My Life as a Matador (Autobiography of Carlos Arruza)

Nonfiction

Learning to Write Fiction From the Masters
The World of Herb Caen
Snoopy's Guide to the Writing Life (with Monte Schulz)
Name Dropping
The Complete Guide to Writing Fiction
Hemingway's Spain
Time Is All We Have
A Revolting Transaction
Fun While It Lasted
How to Fight a Bull
Encyclopedia of Bullfighting
Tahiti
Famous Last Words
San Francisco—A Profile in Words and Pictures
Death of Manolete
Gates of Fear
La Fiesta Brava

HF

Last Boat to Cadiz

Barnaby Conrad

CAPRA PRESS
MEMORABLE BOOKS SINCE 1969
SANTA BARBARA

Last Boat to Cadiz is a work of fiction. Names, places, characters, and incidents are either products of the author's imagination or used to further same. Any resemblance to actual events or to persons alive or dead is coincidental.

A Robert Bason Book
Published by Capra Press
815 De La Vina Street
Santa Barbara, CA 93101
www.caprapress.com

Jacket and book design by Frank Goad.
Illustrations by Barnaby Conrad.

LIBRARY OF CONGRESS CATALOGING-IN-PUBLICATION DATA

Conrad, Barnaby, 1922-
Last boat to Cadiz / by Barnaby Conrad.
p. cm.
"A Robert Bason book."
ISBN 1-59266-032-0 (trade) — ISBN 1-59266-033-9 (numbered hardcover)
— ISBN 1-59266-034-7 (lettered hardcover)
1. Spain—History—1939-1975—Fiction. 2. Americans—Spain—Fiction.
3. Seville (Spain)—Fiction. 4. Consuls—Fiction. I. Title.
PS3553.O515L37 2003
813'.54—dc21
2003005247

10 9 8 7 6 5 4 3 2 1

First Edition

For Shelly Lowenkopf, magician.

Author's Note

Recently I had a telephone call from Spain from Aline, the Countess of Romanones. She was calling from her modest castle in Trujillo.

"Lordy," she said in her still young-sounding voice, "weren't we lucky to have been there then!"

She was referring to the World War II years, when she and I were both in Spain under the aegis of the State Department. She wasn't a countess then, not by a long shot. She was Aline Griffith, a gorgeous young model in her early twenties from Pearl River, New York, who had been recruited by the head of the O.S.S., wild Bill Donavan himself, for spy work in Spain. At that time in 1945, I was the 23-year-old American Vice Consul in Malaga, when I received a phone call early one Sunday morning from the Madrid embassy.

"One of our employees has been put in a Malaga jail – some trouble with her Card of Transit – get her out!"

I got her out. (She wrote about the incident in her fascinating autobiography of a dozen years ago called *The Spy Wore Red.*) I assumed she was a secretary and nothing more. Later I learned she'd been on a very important secret assignment at the time she was jailed and was a high-positioned operator whose code name was Tiger – that one time she'd been forced to kill a man in performance of her duties.

After the war, Aline married Luis Quintanilla of the noble and very wealthy house of Romanones and raised three children. She now takes care of her several domiciles in Spain and America, leads a quiet but busy life, and writes.

Yet it's those three tumultuous war years in Spain she talks so lovingly about. I am the same way. It is hard to explain how colorful, exciting, and occasionally dangerous "neutral" Spain was in that era; the closest thing I can compare it to would be to the film *Casablanca,* with its Nazi villains, American heroes, beautiful women, and spies. And intrigue, always intrigue.

In this book, I've done my best to recreate twenty-four hours in 1945 in Sevilla at the very end of the war.

Most of the names and incidents are fictitious, but the setting is *my* Andalucia, as authentic as I can reproduce it after so many decades.

BARNABY CONRAD
Carpinteria, California
2003

Background

"As a trusted aide of Adolf Hitler's, Martin Bormann was with him in the Berlin bunker when the dictator and Eva Braun killed themselves on April 30, 1945. Loyally, Bormann helped take the bodies outside and burn them in the shell-blasted garden. The next night he and others of the staff made their way through tunnels to a railway station, then walked beside German tanks through the firelit streets. One of the group later testified that he had seen Bormann lying on the ground, unwounded but not breathing. The Nuremberg war-crimes tribunal, unconvinced, sentenced him to death *in absentia*.

Rumors circulated that a submarine had carried him to South America. Simon Wiesenthal, the well-known pursuer of Nazi war criminals, believes that Bormann had exchanged Nazi loot for false passports and a new identity in Argentina and then in Chile.

He had the best of reasons for staying out of sight."
—HUGH TREVOR-ROPER, The Last Days of Hitler

"Paul Hesslein, a pre-war member of our parliament, who had known my father well for years, says he met up with three riders on the Chilean border in the early 1970s and was sure one of them was my father, particularly as he heard him say, 'Wasn't that Hesslein?'"
—MARTIN BORMANN, JR., in an interview in 1990

"To win this war, I need Bormann!"
—ADOLF HITLER, 1943

"I hope the bastard fries in hell!"
—HERMANN GOERING, 1945

"March 1946: American intelligence looks for Bormann in Spain."
—CHARLES WHITING, The Hunt for Martin Bormann

"1946: The hunt for Martin Bormann became the biggest manhunt the world has ever known."
—Ibid

"July 1947: Rumors reach Europe that Bormann is living at the foot of the Andes."

—Ibid

"Bormann was a born survivor. If anyone got out, it would be he."

—ALBERT SPEER, 1971

"Let the suspicion linger that the second most powerful Nazi leader is still alive as a reminder not to forget the horrors of the Third Reich."

—DR. BRODERICH, head of the Berlin CIA, 1953

Andalucia

0	miles	30
0	km 30	

Portugal

Las Marismas

Guadalquivir

San Lúcar de Barrameda

Jerez de la Frontera

Cádiz

Atlantic Ocean

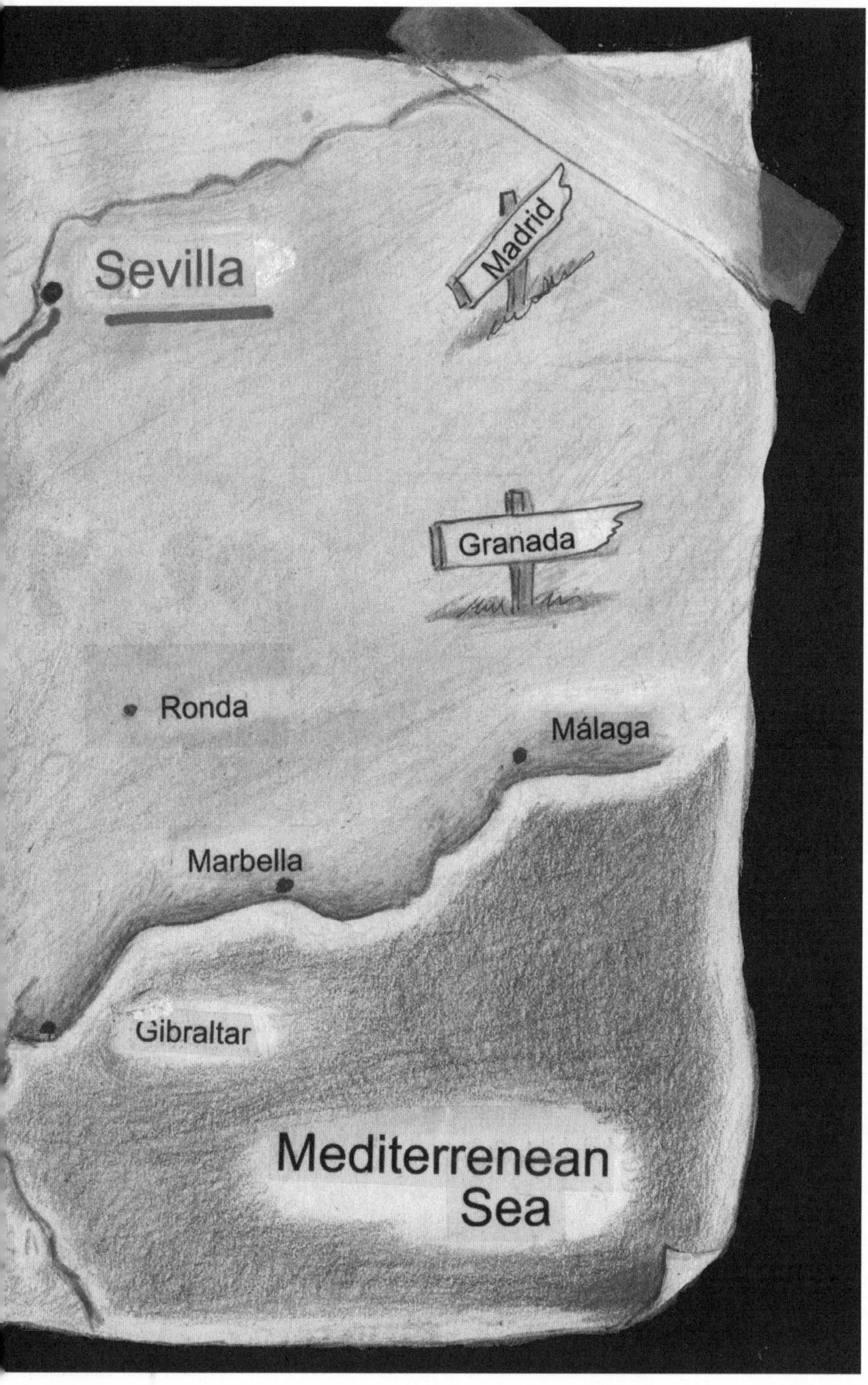
Sevilla
Madrid
Granada
Ronda
Málaga
Marbella
Gibraltar
Mediterrenean
Sea

Last Boat to Cadiz

1

May 3, 1945
Near St. Pierre, France

The old peasant woman wheezed into the farmhouse kitchen, plunking her bag of leeks on the table where the two men, her husband and the stranger, sat with their morning glasses of *café au lait*.

"They are saying in the market," she panted, sagging onto a chair, "that Adolf Hitler is dead! I do not believe it. You will see. Hitler is not dead."

Her husband, in smock and beret, pulled at his white mustache. "Goddamn Germans." He puffed on his pipe.

"Goddamn Hitler!"

The other man, a stranger dressed in expensive city clothes, merely blinked his mesmerizing blue eyes but said nothing as he finished his coffee.

"They say the war will be over in a few days," said the woman, adding bitterly, "*Les sales Boches.* They killed our son, our only son. They killed him early in the war."

"I am sorry to hear that," said the man in French, roughly pronounced with a guttural German accent. "Truly sorry, *madame et monsieur.*"

She turned to him, grateful for his kind words, this charming stranger who had come through the apple orchard to their house late last night, knocked on the door, car broken down, and asked to sleep on the sofa. "And you, *monsieur*, you say you are Swiss? Then you must be glad that the dirty Germans are brought to their knees at last, eh?"

The man managed to smile slightly. "Kismet, *madame*, kismet."

She did not know the word, but she smiled her toothless smile.

"Now I go," the stranger said, abruptly rising from the table. "My...my relatives are expecting me in Spain." He was a stocky, powerful man. The expensive, travel-stained suit he wore did not fit him well; the Swiss businessman he had killed to obtain it, in the bathroom of the Strasbourg train station, had been somewhat smaller.

"But your car, *monsieur!*" said the woman.

"Uh, yes," he said. "My car."

"Didn't you say it broke down a few miles away?"

"I shall come back for it." He turned to the old man. "You say I can walk to the border?"

"*Mais oui, monsieur,*" he answered. "It is very close by." He drew a blue card out of his pocket. "Of course, you have one of these." He shook his head. "Very strict – they won't let you across without a Card of Transit."

The stranger barely hesitated. "I have one, of course." Then: "Is it possible – can you show me a shortcut?"

"*Avec plasir.*" The old man boosted himself up and limped to the door. "Follow me."

The stranger took his raincoat off a hook and put it on, then the homburg hat. "*Madame,*" he made a slight bow, "I thank you for your hospitality."

"*Rien, rien!*" said the woman. She handed him an apple. "For the journey, *monsieur.*"

He clicked his heels in gratitude and followed her husband out the door. The old man walked surprisingly fast. They went down, and then up the path that wound through the dense orchard. After a mile, they came out of the trees, into a clearing on a little hill. The Frenchman stopped and pointed down.

"There, *monsieur,* there you have Spain. Irún, to be exact. You will have no problem, *monsieur,* being Swiss, and with your Card of Transit. You are sure you have one?"

"Of course."

"Good!"

"*Monsieur,* you have been of greater help than you can

know." The stranger reached into the pocket of his rain-coat and drew out a Lüger. From the other pocket he took out the silencer.

The Frenchman smiled uncomprehendingly. "A pistol, *monsieur?*"

"Yes," said the man, screwing the silencer onto the barrel of the pistol. "A gift from a friend."

He stood in front of the old Frenchman and carefully raised the gun to the man's throat.

The old man still didn't understand. Then he felt the cold barrel against the base of his neck, and he heard the stranger say in his native German, *"Auf Wiedersehen,"* and he heard the *pumpff* of the pistol, and for a very brief moment, a fraction of a second, the old man understood.

The stranger carefully bypassed the town of Irún. At a brisk pace he reached Pescadero before dusk. It was a fishing village not far from what was left of the town of Güernica, bombed to extinction by Hitler eight years before during Spain's civil war.

The stranger, the German, wore the beret and smock of the old Frenchman now, but it was an imperfect and uncomfortable disguise; the small garment was barely knee length and revealed the German's tailored trousers and hand-crafted dress shoes. They were his own shoes, very expensive shoes, not those of the man he'd killed in Strasbourg. Also, there was a large splotch of dried blood on the front of the smock, which the German tried to cover with his hand and forearm whenever he passed a villager.

After passing an occasional field-worker who stopped from his planting to wave a greeting, the German began to relax. Then he saw a villager approaching him from the opposite direction.

"*Zigeuner,*" he thought. *Well, we got rid of a lot of them, didn't we? But not enough. A million?*

The villager, a tall youth, a simple Gypsy by the dark look of him, trod lightly over the rock-strewn path, and stopped when he drew abreast of the German. He pointed at his shoes and smiled. "*Lindos los zapatos aquellos.*"

The German didn't understand. He fingered the Lüger in his pocket, wishing he'd left the silencer in place. But, why bother, he didn't want to kill the boy, even if he was a Gypsy, especially out here in the open.

The German smiled, tossed the apple given him by his recent hostess to the youth, and strode on. In another quarter-hour he reached a cobbled street, which led to the quay of the fishing village.

He strode down the street along which the small boats were either in their slips already or were being eased into them. The fishermen's chattering women and lively children were gathering there, to help with the catch from the Bay of Biscay and to scrub down the boats. Some of the boats had big lights on their prows to attract the *chanquete* fish, and they would be going out again when night fell.

The air was salty, fishy, and pungent with the black-tobacco cigarettes that the men and even the women and teenagers smoked. Everyone was too busy to pay much attention to the German, though occasionally he would get the glances that any stranger in this non-tourist village would receive.

Ahead he saw a sign, with a crude bull's head in faded yellow, which read *El Toro Dorado*.

It was clearly the kind of bar he wanted; it would probably cater to the type of person he was looking for.

He crossed the street and walked through the open door. It was dark inside, and as his eyes adjusted to the gloom he saw two old men sitting at a table, playing chess by the light of a candle in a bottle. A wooden fan turned slowly on a smoke-blackened ceiling. Three fishermen hunched over their beers at the zinc bar, apparently arguing over the lottery results in a newspaper. A fat woman, her neck disfigured by a goiter, sat on a stool behind the bar, smoking a pencil-thin cigar.

The smells! How different were the odors of Spain compared to the France he'd just left and even more different from those of his native Germany. Here it was the acrid stench of bad tobacco, *Anís del Mono*, ersatz coffee, saffron, and frying olive oil, everywhere frying olive oil, and cloying sherry wine.

He went to the farthest part of the bar, away from the light from the open door, and sagged down onto a stool. It felt good, so good, to sit down. He'd had very little sleep the last three days. The little Fiesler-Storch reconnaissance plane, perhaps the last of the tiny, two-seater "air taxi cabs" left in Berlin, had gotten him out miraculously, made it all the way to Strasbourg, where it coughed twice, ran out of gas, and bounced down hard on a soccer field. He had hated to kill the pilot, not only a good kid of nineteen but his cousin's youngest son, but dammit, the youth would talk, the Americans would make him talk.

Now the woman humped herself off the stool and came down to him. His Spanish was non-existent, but over the years in his dealings with Mussolini's representatives he'd picked up a smattering of Italian which he'd added to some bits of Pétain French.

He smiled at the woman.

"Bella sera," he said. *"Biere, per piacere."*

"You English?" she grunted.

"Yes," he said. "How did you know?"

"I espeak English," she said.

"Good," he said.

She plunked a glass of dark ale and a little plate of sliced *jamón serrano* in front of him. He extracted a large roll of French francs from his trouser pocket and peeled off some bills.

The woman frowned. "No got Espanish money?"

The German peeled off another bill.

The woman shook her head. "Espanish money worth more than French."

The German pulled two more bills from the roll.

The woman nodded and scooped up the money.

The German drank and casually looked over the three fishermen down the bar. Two were young and short. The third with the blue woolen cap, was husky and easily as tall as the German.

"*Signora,*" said the German haltingly, "*Mio carro,*" he couldn't think of the Italian or Spanish word for broken, and said, "*mio carro e kaput.*"

Offended, she snapped, "Already tol' you. I espeak English."

"Yes, of course," said the German. "My car, it has broken down. I need to have it pushed to a mechanic. I steer," he pantomimed. "Someone push. Would that big chap down there," he peeled off several bills, "be willing to help me?"

She took the bills. "Maybe."

The German smiled and put down another bill for her. "Would you ask him?"

"Can not," she said. "Can not ask. He is a *mudo.*"

"*Mudo?*"

"How you say? Dumb and deaf."

She took a stub of a pencil and wrote some words on a napkin. Then she waddled down to the big fisherman, showed the note to him, and handed him the bills. He looked over at the German with a wide friendly grin and nodded his head twice.

"Thank you, *signora,*" said the German. "And by the way, where is the train station, in case I have to take one?"

"Five estreets," she jabbed a fat finger. "Tha' way."

The German motioned the fisherman to follow him as he left the bar.

They walked two blocks away from the quay. The streetlights were coming on now. On the left the German saw a narrow alley connecting two parallel streets. The dark passageway was deserted, as the people of the town were down at the boats. The German gestured for the fisherman to go first, and the man obeyed with a smile.

When the mute had gone halfway through the alley, the German yanked out his Lüger, lunged at his back, and crashed the butt of the pistol at the base of his skull. The big man staggered, then sagged silently to the cobblestones, like a steer slugged by a sledgehammer in a slaughterhouse.

The German began stripping the unconscious form of its outer clothing, but it was not easy getting the big arms out of the jacket. Leaving the man in his underclothes, the German quickly shed the Frenchman's smock and beret and put on the fisherman's knitted cap, jacket, and rough trousers. But the boots...the German saw that the big man had the feet of a teenage girl. He scooped up some mud and rubbed it on his shoes, but he couldn't change their shape.

He screwed the silencer into his Lüger, held it to the fallen man's ear, and pulled the trigger. The body jumped with the impact. The German lingered only long enough to unscrew the silencer and put it and the pistol in the pockets of the jacket.

Then he hurried down the alley toward the train station. Except for the shoes, his disguise was convincing now; the clothes fit remarkably well, and there was no blood on them. As he walked, he looked at his watch automatically and hummed a little song from his youth.

"*Eine Seefahrt die is lustig, eine Seefahrt die is schön*...how jolly is an outing on the ocean, how very, very jolly..."

He would get to Cadiz on time. And it *would* be a jolly outing on the ocean. The Atlantic Ocean off of Spain.

The same German was in the Sevilla train station twenty-seven hours later. Unshaven and grimy, dressed like a fisherman from the north of Spain, he hurried unnoticed out of the crowded station into the bright Andalucian sun.

Outside awaited a line of open horse-drawn taxis. He strode to one of them, showed the coachman an address written on a scrap of paper, and stepped in the cab. The cabbie touched his visored hat, whacked the skinny horse's flanks with his whip, and the cab clopped through the cobbled streets of the old city. It finally stopped in front of a modern apartment. The cabbie frowned at the offer of French money, and once again the German had to overcompensate.

He went up to the front door and knocked. An attractive blonde woman in her late twenties opened the door as far as its chain bolt would allow. "Yes?"

He spoke softly in German. "Let me in, Mia."

The woman gasped, and her fist went to her mouth. "I heard on the radio that you were dead!"

"Let me in!" he commanded.

"My daughter's here. And a friend of mine is due any

moment. Please go!"

"You wouldn't turn away a relative," he said. "Would you, Fraulein von Wurmbrandt?"

"You are no relative!" she said, and tried to close the door.

But he had his foot there to block its closing all the way.

"I am still your godfather," he said. "I have something here from your brother."

"Max–" she said. "He's well? You have something from Max? Tell me!"

"Right here." He patted the thick jacket. "He said it was important. Open the door, *liebchen*. It is too big to–"

"Leave it for me at the German Consulate," she said.

He gave a breathy laugh. "Dear Mia, don't you realize we have lost the war? The consulates will be taken over by the British and Americans. I can't go near them. Open the door. We are Germans, you and I!"

"*I* am a German," she said. "*You* are a Nazi!"

"Open the door."

"You are an embarrassment! Why don't you go for asylum to your good old friend, General Franco? He loves Nazis."

"Not since we started losing," he said. "Let me in!"

"No."

He sighed.

"All right," he said softly. "I will go, God knows to where."

He turned and started to walk away.

"Wait," she said. "The thing from Max."

He turned back and put his hand in his jacket. "It won't fit through the opening. Take off the chain."

She hesitated and bit her lower lip.

"You swear – you really have something from Max?"

He nodded solemnly.

"What is it?" she said.

"I don't know," he said. "It is wrapped. He said it was very important." He turned to go again.

She slid the chain of the bolt back and opened the door a little wider. "Just hand me the–"

The man hurled his bulk at the door, slamming the woman back into the hall. Inside, he kicked the door closed with his heel as he drew the pistol from his jacket.

"Max has been dead for a month," he said. "He was a traitor to the Reich. We were forced to hang him on a meat hook." He shook his head. "Stupid, stupid girl!"

2

Across the city of Sevilla, this day had started badly for Wilson Tripp, the twenty-three-year-old American Vice Consul. As usual, he was at his desk in the Consulate on the beautiful Avenida Paseo de las Delicias that ran along the Guadalquivir River.

First, the letter that landed on his desk before noon. It was misspelled and addressed simply: *Al Vise Council Americano.* Inside, the writing was crude, like a ransom note.

"*Señor:* you will die this week when the great Third Reich dies. Death to all enemies of General Franco! Sleep on your elbow, *señor!*"

It was unsigned, but Wilson knew it was from López, a sleazy character who had threatened him before. He'd caught López shipping strategic war materials, namely wolfram for the manufacture of steel, to the Germans; apparently, it had ruined the man's reputation, whatever that might have been. The letter upset Wilson more than frightened him.

Wilson hadn't wanted to ruin López. Nothing personal; he'd just wanted to keep him from sending any more aid to the Nazis.

He asked the American secretary and the Spanish clerks if they had seen who had delivered the letter. They hadn't. The office boy had shrugged: "A lady left it on the counter."

Wilson tried to dismiss the letter from his mind as he sorted the dull State Department mail that had just come in the diplomatic pouch through the courier from Madrid. He thought of showing the letter to the Consul, but asked himself why? Tottle would just make a big thing of it, write all sorts of dispatches to the Department and waste everyone's time.

Wilson's mind was on a more important subject: How to save a little girl's life. A little German girl.

For months, years, Allied bombs had been killing German civilians, and here in Spain he was trying to save one unimportant young German life. And he could tell no one about it; it would ruin his career in the Foreign Service, a career his family put such store by.

He picked up the phone and gave the operator the number. It rang twice, then Mia's cool voice came on. Only a trace of German accent, but he sensed tension in her voice.

"Wilson! Are we still going..."

"Don't," Wilson warned. "Not on the phone. Everything as planned." He hung up.

Just before lunch the dapper Consul, Caleb Tottle, came out of his office. Tottle boasted that he had a collection of over four hundred ties – cravats he called them – and never wore the same one twice in a year. He dressed as he had so many years ago at Harvard, where he'd been voted Best Dressed and Best Bridge Player and Most Musical. Or so he claimed.

"Tripp!" His mustache twitched and he spoke in conspiratorial tones. "When you're downtown, cruise around, keep your eye out for any strangers."

"Strangers?" Wilson asked.

"Anyone conspicuously different – like a Nazi in disguise."

You've got to be kidding, Wilson thought. "Sir, what does a Nazi in disguise look like?"

"How the hell should I know?" growled Tottle. "Just try following orders for a change!" He went back into his office and slammed the door.

Wilson's relationship with his superior had started badly on his first day at work six months ago in the Consul's office.

"So you're Tripp," the Consul had greeted him. "Knew your father in the State Department years ago. Can't say I liked him. Drank a lot."

Wilson burned inwardly and said nothing.

"So you're a Yale man," Tottle said.

"Yes, sir."

"Well," Tottle purred. "We can't all go to the school of our first choice, can we?"

Wilson gave a wan smile at the joke. "I might have gone to Harvard, sir, with pleasure – but they didn't offer me the scholarship that Yale did."

"No money, eh?"

A few minutes later Consul Tottle had pointed at his wastepaper basket and ordered: "Kindly empty that."

Foolishly, Wilson had snapped: "Sir, I'm a Foreign Service officer."

Tottle had eyed him coolly, with a small derisive smile. "Well, then," he said, "you should be able to handle the assignment."

Wilson emptied the wastepaper basket.

In the ensuing months, the relationship had not improved; there seemed to have been some unresolved grudge with Wilson's father in the past.

Now, as Wilson started to leave the Consulate, Moriarity, the chief clerk, lurched in. Older than Wilson but lower in status in the Foreign Service, he and Wilson were good friends. His Irishness came and went, often dictated by the flow of Irish whiskey from the ever-present silver flask.

"Where you going, bucko?" Moriarity asked with a Boston-Irish accent.

"Where you been?" countered Wilson. "As Raymond Chandler said, you've got a breath on you that would start the windmill in an old Dutch painting."

"A pox on you," said Moriarity. "Where you going?"

"Out," said Wilson.

"And may the wind at yer back not be of yer own makin'," said Moriarity, using the heavy accent of his father, a Cork man.

Wilson managed to grin; Moriarity was all right. But Wilson's mind was on something else. He stood up from the desk and walked out of the office, his limp barely noticeable. One might have thought he merely had a sore foot; few would recognize that he had to wear a brace for a shattered knee, the result of a youthful indiscretion, "the unpleasantness," as his mother always called it, "in Mexico City."

Wilson went out on the river side of the building where the maroon Consulate limousine awaited. Wilson was in the back seat before Pepe, the chauffeur, could open the door for him.

"Where to, *señor*?"

"Across the river, Pepe," Wilson said. "To the boat again."

Pepe was a terrible driver; he stopped at corners that had no stop signs and didn't stop at those that did. He let Wilson off at the banks of the Guadalquivir, the large, slow-moving river that started somewhere near Córdoba and, after four hundred miles, ended in the Atlantic near Cadiz.

Captain Nacho Pérez was standing by the gangplank of his small boat.

"*Buenos días*," said Wilson.

"*El parné*," was the man's grunted reply, in Gypsy slang. "The money." He was scruffy, with a gray stubble, a dirty undershirt, a beret pulled down to bloodshot eyes, a bent cigarette glued to the lower lip. His body smelled like a pet shop and his breath was perfumed with the smell of *Anís del Mono*.

"*Tenga*," Wilson said and held up two one hundred-dollar bills. Nacho's eyes narrowed perceptibly. Wilson tore the bills in half. "You'll get the other halves in Cadiz tomorrow."

Nacho shrugged and grunted: "And if we don't reach Cadiz, *señor*?"

"What do you mean?"

"Bad enough before," the man scowled. "Now Franco, he's in Sevilla. His soldiers, police – they're all over the place."

"You're armed," said Wilson, "I assume."

The captain said, "*Hombre!* Just give me all the money now, for God's sake! I give it to my wife to keep. In case I don't come back."

Wilson hesitated. He took out another hundred-dollar bill and gave it to the man whole. "Give her this."

Nacho's mouth widened in a grotesque smile, revealing several brown-centered stubs aligned with two gold teeth; Wilson was reminded of an etching from Goya's *Disparates*.

"I shall give it to my widow," he said, pocketing the money.

"At seven, then," said Wilson.

The captain gave a half-salute. "*A su disposición*, Señor Consul. How many will there be?"

"Two. Only two."

"You are not coming with us?"

"No. Just the woman and her child – the sick child."

"There are other passengers."

"Who?"

The man shrugged. "The American *torero* and some old American woman."

Wilson noticed the girl for the first time. She was sitting on the deck playing with a kitten. A womanly fifteen, barefoot, dressed in corduroy trousers and a man's shirt. She probably was the captain's daughter.

He thought of the *piropo* he'd recently heard on Sierpes Street; a Sevillano man had whistled and said to a passing beauty: "*Tantas curvas y yo sin frenos* – so many curves and me without brakes!" Wilson loved the Andalucians and their colorful speech.

She gave Wilson a long look, a mysterious half-smile and an arched eyebrow. She was tawny, as cat-like as the animal she was playing with.

"Don't celebrate too soon, *capitán*," said Wilson. "You can drink when you get to Cadiz."

"God says 'better drunk than sick,'" said Nacho. "*Mejor borracho que enfermo.*"

"Funny, never heard Him say that," Wilson said. He

turned and walked toward the Consular car. The air smelled like damp dust; this was the way it was in Andalucia just before a rain and with the sun still shining.

It was going to work, thought Wilson as he mounted the steps in the street. The car was waiting.

Pepe, the uniformed chauffeur, held the door open for him.

But Franco! He'd forgotten about Franco's men.

"Where to, *señor*?" Pepe asked.

Why's it going to work?

"Back across the bridge," Wilson said.

Because it had to work.

He got in the back seat and they drove away from the dock.

"Nice day," said the driver; with his Sevilla accent and congenital stammer, he was virtually unintelligible.

"Go past the tobacco factory," said Wilson. "I'll tell you where to stop."

As the car headed toward the bridge linking Triana with its big sister, Sevilla, Wilson looked back at the *Cayetana*. The small boat rocked gently at her mooring as a freighter glided by, roiling the water of the Guadalquivir. The *Cayetana*, about forty feet long, wasn't much to look at, with its peeling paint, snubbed prow, and the grubby fender tires along its sides, but it was the best he could get on such short notice. After all, no one was asking the craft to sail across the Atlantic, or even over the straits from Gibraltar to Tangier; all she had to do was go about sixty-five miles down the river, as she did several times a week to pick up fish from Cadiz and load smuggled goods. Only this time the contraband cargo would be exclusively human.

Wilson could see the captain washing down the decks with buckets of water.

Gilded in the late afternoon sun, the *Cayetana* and the small craft next to it made a nice picture postcard, a typical glimpse of the *Wadi al-KebiR,* as the Moors had named it some ten centuries earlier, "The Great River." The Guadalquivir was the biggest in Spain, a river of history, of violence and glory. "A river of lions," Garcia Lorca had called it.

There are certain names – geographic, hotels, rivers, islands – that reek of romance and adventure and make one tingle by their very sound. As a daydreaming boy in San Francisco, Wilson had made an ever-expanding list of them: Tanganyika, Claridge's, Macchu Pichu, Raffles, Salonika, Big Timber, Sparta, Bora Bora, Stonehenge, Madagascar, Istanbul, Kashmir, Khyber, the Yukon, the Thames, Katmandu, the Umpqua, Odessa, the Euphrates, Taos, the Congo.

It was a long list, but of all the names he'd vowed one day to visit in quest of adventure, he'd only managed so far to see the Guadalquivir. And this day, this fine spring day in sunny Spain, Wilson feared there would be more than enough adventure to satisfy him.

As they drove along the river's teeming bank, a string of belled donkeys laden with firewood strolled in front of the car, ears flapping rhythmically. The owner, in a beret, idly beat at them with a long stick, regular as a metronome. Triana was predominantly Gypsy, and the smells in the narrow street were dung, urine, wine, over-ripe melons, and the sting of black-tobacco cigarettes. The acrid scent of coffee made from acorns these days wafted from the sidewalk café, La Querencia, mingling with the sweet smell of flowers. One old *churros* vendor clutched a baby with a carnation taped to its bald head. There were no "Nazis in disguise" around, as far as Wilson could see.

Radio Andorra, out of reach of Franco's censorship, Spain's only semi-unbiased news source, was muttering from under the dashboard of the limousine.

"Turn it up, Pepe," Wilson said.

"*Sí, señor.*" From Pepe's mouth it came out "Thee th-th-thenyoh."

The radio said nothing new, just that Manolete had cut ears at Ronda again. At the Consulate, Wilson usually received dispatches before Radio Andorra, but he listened to the woman's crackling, nasal voice: "While Hitler and Goebbels have been dead several days, apparent suicides, the war goes on as the Allies seek an unconditional surrender. Himmler, von Ribbentrop, Speer, and Goering are in custody. Martin Bormann, chief of the Nazi Party since 1941 and Hitler's right-hand man since 1943, has been reported killed by the Russians outside of Hitler's bunker. General Franco is in Sevilla to address the Falangista Party and the Spanish public tomorrow."

The car turned and entered the bridge. Ahead lay

Sevilla, clean, serene, and majestic compared to the cacophony and filthy disarray of Triana. At the end of the bridge squatted Columbus's Tower of Gold, the small octagonal fort where the explorer was said to have stored his New World treasures. Behind that, the great monolithic minaret of the Giralda thrust up into the warm spring sky, reminding the world that Sevilla was, and would be forever, Moorish. Over to the left was the Maestranza, Sevilla's ancient bullring, where only last Sunday Wilson had seen the great Manolete and the Mexican Arruza perform in an historic *corrida;* the fact that the world was in turmoil hadn't affected *la fiesta brava* in Spain.

Wilson still loved bullfighting, the essence of everything Spanish, in spite of the fact that he'd almost lost his leg to a bull three years earlier. The summer of his freshman year at Yale, he'd gone to the University of Mexico's summer school to study painting. During his second month there, he'd bumped into a friend from Yale, a South American architectural student from Bogotá named Jaime, an amiable, fat intellectual, who insisted they go to a *corrida.* All Wilson knew about bullfighting was what he'd learned from *Death in the Afternoon,* but the pageantry and color appealed to his artistic senses. Killing the bulls didn't seem so bad to him; after all, the ones chosen for the bullring lived twice as long as the ones selected for the slaughterhouse. Jaime was a drinker, and instead of red wine in his leather *bota,* he had tequila.

Wilson was leery of any alcoholic beverages, having

been long alerted to the dangers by his hard-drinking father's behavior and setbacks. But Jaime had pressed the *bota* on him again and again. And, after all, they were in Mexico.

After a couple of swigs, Wilson determined – most rationally, it seemed – that bullfighting looked easy. "The poor dumb bull just keeps going at the whatchamacallit."

"*El capote,*" said Jaime.

"Right! Because it's dumb."

"Because the man is an expert," said Jaime.

"It goes at the cape because it's red," said Wilson.

"No," said Jaime, "the cape is yellow on one side, and the animal charges just as hard as at the red side. The bull is colorblind and goes at the cape because the man stays still himself but moves the cape skillfully in front of the bull's head."

"It's not fair," said Wilson. "It's so easy to fool the poor animal."

Jaime laughed. If it was so easy, why didn't Wilson try it? On the last bull of the afternoon, Wilson grabbed his raincoat, jumped down out of the stands, vaulted the *barrera* fence, and confronted the bull, holding his raincoat as he'd seen the *matador* do. The crowd gasped and the bullfighters shouted for him to retreat. The bull charged. Now it seemed bigger than a Greyhound bus as it hurtled toward him. Standing still, Wilson swung his raincoat and the wicked horns sliced past. He'd been spared!

"*Olé!*" shouted the crowd, bemused that a *gringo* would spontaneously try their ancient sport. Here, truly, was a unique *espontáneo*. Wheeling, the bull charged back at Wilson. Again he managed to make the animal's horns go at the cloth and not his body. Then the crowd's shouts became screams as the bull, on its return charge, veered into Wilson's body. A horn stabbed in and out of Wilson's right knee, and he pinwheeled to the sand. He was carried out semiconscious. After an hour in the bullring's infirmary, he was rushed to Mexico's best hospital. The next day the newspapers ran the story of "the *gringo espontáneo*." Two top *toreros* visited him in the hospital, and he enjoyed a brief celebrity.

After a three-month recovery back in San Francisco, he returned to Yale with a leather, metal, and cloth brace on his knee. While he graduated with honors, he could not be accepted into the military. He joined the Foreign Service in Washington, D.C., as a clerk in the State Department. After some training, and because of his fluency in Spanish, he was sent to Sevilla as a Vice Consul. And even though the memory of the goring was still painful, here in Spain he'd gone to several of the *tienta* parties given by the prominent bull breeders at their elegant ranches around Sevilla. At these festive occasions, the young animals, little more than calves, were tested for bravery, and guests were invited to go down to the small arenas and demonstrate their own bravery and skill with a cape. When he was first handed a cape at the Benítez Cubero Ranch, he wasn't sure his trembling hands could swing it in front of the small but vicious animal. But he went out into the arena and amazed the audience, and himself, with his awkward, but efficacious handling of the furious little animal's charges. The next time he did better, and felt he was actually learning the intricate science of tauromachy from the professional *matadors* who were always present at these events.

But his boss, Consul Tottle, had said bullfighting, even with calves, was undignified for a Vice Consul and forbade him to participate in any more *tientas*.

Now, after six months of carefully trying to follow the rules and procedures of the Consular Corps, he was about to commit an act that might prove even more dangerous than his brief bullfighting episodes.

Today on Sevilla's streets they drove by groups of Spanish soldiers on every corner, automatic weapons slung over their shoulders. And everywhere in patrolling pairs were the feared Guardia Civil, the ruthless rural police, with their patent-leather, three-cornered hats.

The car drove past the elegant tiled Alfonso Trece Hotel, named for the last King of Spain. They sped past the hulking tobacco factory where the prototype for Carmen had worked rolling cigars on her not-so-virginal thighs; it looked more like the annex to a castle than a factory.

"*Aquí,*" said Wilson.

He jumped out of the limousine. "Pepe, go down to the end of Flores Street. Turn left at Almendro and park in the shade. I'll meet you there."

Under the trees and out of the late afternoon sun, the car would be inconspicuous. No need for all of Sevilla to see the American Consulate car, its gold seal on the door, parked in front of a German's apartment, and not just any German – the niece of Hitler's famous cabinet minister.

Wilson walked across the narrow street, conscious of how American he looked in this operetta setting: light hair, in a tie and J. Press seersucker jacket, five inches taller than most of the Spanish men he passed. He was only twenty-three years old, but his hard brown eyes and the furrow between them belonged to a much older man.

Wilson came to the two-story apartment house, modern and nondescript, flanked by buildings whose first occupants might have leaned out of the windows to watch Columbus's ships sail triumphantly up the Guadalquivir.

He stood for a moment, looking up at Mia's apartment. What was wrong? It wasn't a gut feeling or intuition; Wilson was too practical for that. It was something physical.

The windows. The Venetian blinds were shut. This was a first. In the few times he'd surreptitiously visited her apartment – theoretically for the O.S.S. and Embassy war criminal files, but more and more for his own affection and desire for the beautiful German – the blinds had never been shut. And now he thought he saw them opening and someone looking at him from the bedroom window.

Something was wrong. But then it was the right time for things to be wrong. Hitler dead three days now, yet still no cessation to the war in Europe. Chaos and mayhem in Berlin, revengeful madness in the Russian troops, resentment and unrest in predominantly pro-German Spain. Everything topsy-turvy.

He went to the grilled iron gate in front of the door

and opened it. He put his hand on the knob.

"Mia?" he called once. Then louder.

He turned the knob. The door was unlocked – that was unusual. On the other hand, she was expecting him. He opened the door and stepped in cautiously.

There was no one in the small living room. Everything seemed all right, nothing amiss. Flowers everywhere – how she loved flowers. Two tennis rackets in the corner: the small one for her sickly seven-year-old daughter, who might never play again. An easel stood near the dining table with a half-finished, more-than-competent painting of the wild flower fields around Dresden, copied from a postcard. He'd helped her a bit with it, though portraits, not landscape, had been his forte at Yale before the war. The upright piano with the sheet music of "Für Elise" open where one of her pupils had left it. He liked the idea that she took lessons in art and gave lessons in music; his mother played the piano too. They would like each other, Mia and his mother.

A leather wine skin with "Pamplona" branded on its side hung on the kitchen door, a souvenir of her honeymoon with Luis Alvarez, whose handsome photo smiled down from the wall. A lawyer, he was now in his Blue Division uniform, one of the 47,000 Spanish volunteers who were battling the Russians on the German front with Franco's enthusiastic support. She hadn't heard from him for six months, the only word being that the crack Division's casualties "had been enormous." Wilson knew she'd almost given up hope. And he felt badly that he wouldn't mind if she did give up.

Beside him on a table were propped photos of her late mother and father (Dresden), her late younger sister (Dresden), her late older sister (Hamburg), and her Uncle Wilhelm von Wurmbrandt, the high-ranking aristocratic general. "He and Canaris are the only good ones in the whole rotten bunch," the head of the O.S.S. had told Wilson once. The thin-faced general was dressed in mufti. New York and London social circles once lionized this suave diplomat, before he'd been swept into the hypnotic apotheosis of Adolf Hitler. Mia only said the name once to him, but it flowed musically in her beautiful voice: "Fohnvoombrahndt." It was rumored that he'd recently been involved in a plot to kill Hitler and was executed horribly.

Next to the photos stood the ornately carved mahogany hutch, brought from Germany when Mia'd married the Spaniard. In it were plates and tureens and figurines. Wilson didn't know anything about china, but it was obvious that these pieces were "important," as his mother back in San Francisco would say. Of course they *would* be. Mia's family had been prominent in Dresden porcelain for two hundred years until last February thirteenth. Mia told him that she and her younger sister happened to have been visiting their parents that week. Her voice was so flat and cold, tearless and angry, when she spoke about it. It was Sunday, and she'd stayed home alone in their big house up on the hill while the family went down into town to church. They had heard the Allied planes coming in waves and had seen the bright red glow as the firebombing swept through the streets. When she ran down after the air raid, there they all were.

"My family, my friends, the shopkeepers, all lying in the streets and sidewalks dressed in their Sunday best, not burned or bloody, but all brutally shrunk from the heat and much too small for their clothes, and all of them dead, so unnecessarily dead in the most innocent city in Germany."

The cabinet was the same as always. But then Wilson saw it: Over a porcelain rooster was draped a blue knitted fisherman's cap.

"Mia!" he called.

An ancient long-haired dachshund waddled out of the kitchen and rubbed its swayed back against Wilson's legs.

"Good old dog, Schatzi." Wilson crouched and patted it. "Where's your mistress?"

The bedroom door opened, and she came out.

"Here I am," she announced, quickly closing the door behind her. She was tan and wore no makeup, her blonde hair tousled. Dressed in a low-cut peasant blouse and a dirndl, she was so healthy, with natural good looks; she could pass for twenty instead of twenty-eight. He'd become fond of her even though it was forbidden fruit.

"Everything's all set, Mia! Your boat leaves for Cadiz at seven tonight – the *Cayetana*. Triana pier, Captain Pérez–"

"Wilson!" She cut him off, almost harshly, put a finger to her lips, and came toward him. "Bad boy, you haven't even kissed me hello!"

He had never kissed her, although the thought had crossed his mind more than once; but Mia was one of the enemy, "an assignment" from the State Department, and she was very much married to her missing husband.

Now, astonishingly, she put her arms around him and kissed him hard on the mouth.

She broke off the kiss: "So good to see you, dear Wilson." There was something strangely operatic in her gestures, and her eyes darted to an invisible audience.

When he stepped forward to kiss her again, she put her cheek next to his.

"*Cállate! Cuidado!*" she whispered fiercely in Spanish. "Be careful! Be quiet!"

He looked around in confusion. There was no evidence of anyone to be quiet for. Except in the hutch, where the fisherman's cap covered the porcelain rooster. He pointed at it in pantomime. She nodded, and jabbed her finger toward the bedroom. She took a cigarette with trembling fingers from the silver box on the coffee table.

"Where's Heidi?" he asked casually; it seemed safe enough to ask about her daughter.

"Heidi is," she lit the cigarette with the table lighter. "She is in the bedroom, helping me pack for Madrid." She emphasized the name of the city. "She's very excited about seeing Madrid. You know, the Prado and the Royal Palace and–"

The door to the bedroom opened, and the young girl stood there, very pale, unsteady, like a butterfly that had been forced to become a moth, almost white from the fatal illness. Maybe this new drug would cure her – his brand-new miracle drug. It was called penicillin. So far only the Allied forces had it; clandestinely, Wilson had arranged for Heidi to get the shots courtesy of his friend the Naval attaché in Madrid and the American destroyer that would be off Gibraltar, next to Cadiz, tomorrow.

"Hello, Mr. Tripp!" The seven-year-old was dressed in boots and jodhpurs, though she'd not been well enough to ride her beloved pony for months. Her black eyes were wide with apprehension, and Wilson saw why.

"How do you do, sir?" said a deep voice in strongly accented English.

Behind the girl loomed an imposing figure. He was not tall, but the bulk of his upper body filled the doorway. About forty years old, Tripp thought, dressed like a fisherman from the north of Spain: a black pea jacket and coarse trousers. His face was strong and not unhandsome. The deep-set blue eyes were so pale that there seemed to be no distinction between the pigmentation of the iris and the cornea.

"Your name, sir?" the man asked. In the courtesy was a hard command that belonged to no ordinary fisherman.

"Wilson Tripp. And yours?"

"I am an old friend of Mia," replied the man. "In fact, her godfather. My name is Hans."

There were heavy pouches under the man's eyes, eyes desperately in need of a good night's rest. Wilson saw the tiny red veins in his cheeks, like the silk threads in a dollar bill or, more accurately, in a Deutschmark.

"Sit," the man said quietly to Mia and her daughter. They sat on the couch. Mia put her arm around the child protectively.

"So!" he said. It sounded like "zoh." He stood over Mia. "Dear goddaughter, you tell me you are packing to go to Madrid, but now I hear Mr. Tripp say you are going to Cadiz instead. Why did you not tell me, *liebchen?*"

Mia raised her head and made eye contact. "We go to Cadiz first," she said. "Then to Madrid."

The man paced and rubbed his mustache and four-day beard, and, Wilson imagined, if he had held a riding crop he would have slapped his thigh as he walked. He was not fat, but thick and strong. Those powerful legs might have followed after beaters flushing grouse, Wilson thought, or climbed Bavarian alps after stag, or goose-stepped for miles on end, but he hadn't developed those muscles striding the deck of a fishing trawler. "I have never been to Spain before," the man said, talking like a visiting lecturer, "but always good marks I had in geography at the academy. I learned early never to go south when you mean to go north. Your itinerary, *liebchen,* sounds like going to Berlin from Vienna via Lisbon, *nicht wahr?*"

Mia did not stammer, saying quickly: "We must get some special medicine from Gibraltar for Heidi. It will make her well, they say. Then we go to Madrid. For vacation."

He sat down in the overstuffed chair, letting out a critical sigh. "And why do you not tell me you go to Cadiz? Is it because you know I want to go to Cadiz? That I must go to Cadiz? That I *will* go to Cadiz? Why you do not tell me of this boat called what, *Cayetana?*"

The dog rubbed against the German's leg. To Wilson's surprise, the man reached down and stroked the dachshund tenderly.

"It did not seem to be important," Mia said.

"Just so," said the man, continuing to pet the dog.

He looked at his watch – not a fisherman's watch but an expensive-looking Patek Philipe. "You say it leaves at seven, Herr Consul?"

Wilson was startled. "How did you know I was with the Consulate?"

"Elementary, my dear Watson." Though he spoke English fluently, his *w*'s came out more *v*'s. "I saw you just now emerge from a limousine with the Consulate seal on it. I take it you have been spying on my goddaughter for Mister Wild Bill Donovan. I assure you Mia knows nothing of value to your State Department."

Wilson flushed. "Just who the hell are you? What do you want?"

"Do not get with excitement." The man smiled slightly. "Just call me Hans, a good German. Yes, there are good Germans. And what I need from you, my friend, my new enemy-friend, is something important, and I need it right away. You see, your coming here is almost too good to be true."

"So," Wilson said warily, "what is it you need?"

"I need a passport. A very small passport."

"Why not go to the German Consulate, Mr. Good German? It's just down the street."

"Ah, you see, that is not a good idea, not at all.

Perhaps you have heard that the war is virtually over."

"Perhaps."

"And that the wrong side has won?"

"Perhaps not."

"I need a passport from the wrong side, the winning side. You can furnish me with such a one, an American one."

"You must be out of your mind."

"Perhaps," said the man. "But you will get it for me."

Wilson stood. "I will call Consul Schmidt at the German Consulate right now. This is protocol. Then I'll call my Consul and report that an unregistered German citizen has arrived in town and they should inform the authorities."

Wilson started to go to the phone.

"Wilson, no!" Mia warned. "That would be a mistake!"

"The lady is right," said the German quietly, shaking his head. "A terrible mistake."

"Look," Wilson said, "I don't know who you are, Mr. Good German, but you are not a fisherman, and you are not legal. I'm going back to the Consulate and–"

"Don't get with excitement, my friend," said the German.

Wilson did not see the German take out the pistol from his jacket. But there it was, a Lüger suddenly, casually, placed on the coffee table. The German extracted a five-inch cylinder from his pocket.

As the German screwed the silencer onto the pistol's barrel, he fixed his heavy-lidded eyes, a puff adder's eyes, on Wilson.

"You are indeed not going to the German Consul. No, my friend, you are going straight to your own Consulate to get me a passport. Then you will wish me *bon voyage*."

"And if I refuse?"

With his left hand, the German picked up the pistol, yanked back the cocking mechanism, and pointed it carefully, first at Mia and then at the girl. "You say the boat leaves at seven? I assure you if you are not back here by five-thirty, they will both be dead."

The girl moved closer to her mother.

"He means it, Wilson," Mia spoke between clenched teeth. "Please do what he says – for Heidi's sake!"

Wilson's forehead was moist. The gun was pointed at him now; he would have no chance if he tried to wrest it away.

"The Consulate doesn't close until seven," he said. "I couldn't get away any earlier – it would be noticed."

"Six then. You can get here by six?"

"Six-fifteen."

"Six-fifteen exactly," said the German, lowering the pistol. "And do not be rash, do not try to be the big hero. Call no police, confide in no one, leave no clever little notes for people. Be here with a passport appropriate for a man about my age. Ah yes, a small detail but important. I shall want a little gum arabic."

"Gum arabic?"

"Paste. Glue." He put down the pistol. "And most important. Bring the – the how you call it – the..." He brought his fist down on the table twice as a demonstration.

"The seal?" Wilson asked incredulously. "The embosser?"

"Yah, the seal."

"Impossible!" said Wilson. "That's a federal offense!"

"Get it."

"But the Consul keeps the embosser inside the safe, in his own office."

"Get it," said the German.

"It can't be done."

"Get it." He put his hand on the pistol.

Wilson gave Mia a long look. Her face was drawn, impassive, resigned. Then he started for the door.

"Wilson–" she began with hopeless calm.

He stopped.

She shook her head. "Nothing, only that – I am sorry. It is none of my doing."

It was as though she were adding: All of it was none of my doing – the Versailles Treaty, the Third Reich and its war-bent Führer, weak Uncle Wilhelm becoming a top Nazi, Poland and France, choosing this fugitive from wherever for a godparent, my daughter's illness, and you being American and my being German and all – *not my doing!*

"Just so," said the German, patting the pistol. "Six-fifteen o'clock. I shall be looking out the window. If you do not come alone, they die. If you are late, they die. Do not get with excitement. No heroics. And we shall all live happily ever after."

3

Pepe braked the Consulate limousine, allowing two dozen horsemen to cross in front of it. The riders were spectacularly dressed in flowing white robes, and they carried spears with pennants streaming from them. These were members of Franco's crack Moorish guard. The car started up again, and so did Wilson's thoughts.

He was about to do something certainly illegal, maybe even treasonous.

He could almost hear Consul Tottle's refined voice: "Tripp, we have it from reliable sources that this oh-so-nice girl might very well be the agent through whom our most recent oil allotment to Spain ended up on Nazi submarines lying off Cadiz and Huelva."

Who the hell was this "good German" and how had he

gotten into Spain without a passport? He obviously had a German passport but didn't want to use it, even in so-called neutral Spain. He was probably some high official, judging by his manner, his fancy watch, and the fact that he was Mia's godfather. He was also some sort of criminal if he didn't even trust himself to the German Consulate for sanctuary. An innocent German citizen had nothing to fear in Spain, war or no war.

Whoever he was, he was a walking nightmare.

This man was desperate and dangerous. Once he'd gotten what he wanted from Wilson, he could very well kill him. Wilson thought of how his father used to quote, when half loaded, from Marcus Aurelius's *Meditations*: "Ol' Marc said that men shouldn't fear death, whether or not there's an afterlife, 'cause if there is, hey, then we should be joyful to leave this rotten old world for a better one, and if not, all we do is pass into nothingness, and then we're free of all pain and worry."

That, somehow, was no consolation. His only access to a weapon was a one-bladed Army knife his grandfather had given him five Christmases ago, just before his death. "Carried it all through the First World War," he'd said. But it was now in a drawer in his hotel room. Some weapon.

"Stop at the Maria Cristina," he ordered the chauffeur.

Sevilla's second-best hotel was on the way to the Consulate. The chauffeur parked the car in front and Wilson hurried through the empty lobby. He bypassed the slow elevator and strode up the marble stairs to his second-floor room. A fat little chambermaid was making the bed. She smiled a nearly toothless smile. She nodded enthusiastically at the easel in a corner of the large room. Wilson's half-finished painting of the Giralda Tower was on the easel.

"*Bonita, señor,*" the woman said nodding several times for emphasis. "*Muy bonita!*"

"*Gracias,* Josefina," he said. The picture didn't look too bad. He'd learned a lot about light from the Spanish paintings he'd seen in Sevilla and Madrid, especially from Velázquez and Sorolla. If he could only paint sunlight like Sorolla!

He opened the bureau drawer and took out the knife. He put it in a pants pocket. Then he thought: *But supposing he frisks me?*

He turned to the maid. "You may finish that later, Josefina."

When the woman had left, he undid his belt and dropped the trousers around his ankles. He sagged down on the bed and unlaced the leather binding of the knee brace. "Good old Betsy," he said. It still gave him a jolt when he saw the scarred limb.

He patted the brace. "I knew you'd come in handy some day, Betsy," he said. He took the knife from his pocket, wrapped it in a handkerchief, slid it into the side of the brace, laced it up, and pulled up his pants.

When the phone rang, he was startled. Who knew he was here?

"One moment, *señor,*" said the *centralita*, "an overseas

call for you from San Francisco."

There was some crackling, and he heard his mother's voice for the first time in six months.

"What's wrong, Mom?" Calls from the States were so rare.

"It's your birthday. Happy birthday!"

He had totally forgotten.

"I know how terribly busy you are, dear–"

"Is everyone all right at home?" he asked.

"Just fine. No news since my last letter, except Lucy. Lucy Ames is getting married."

Lucy had been a girl friend in high school but meant little to him now. "Give her my best."

"Here's Dad–"

"Hey, old boy!"

He heard his father's deep voice, and he could tell instantly that he'd had two old-fashioneds. Not drunk yet but, well, effusive.

"Happy birthday, and how goes it in sunny Spain? How's the war going? Any *señoritas*?"

"Hi, Dad. Great to hear your voice! You probably know more about the war than we do over here."

He knew what was coming next: "How's the old leg?"

His father always asked that as though there could be a change, as though he were some sort of lizard that could grow a new limb. But Wilson answered: "Played a little tennis last week. Did pretty well." And to change the subject: "How's Maddie?" She'd been his beloved yellow mutt since childhood.

"Awful old, Wilson," said his father. "May have to put her down."

It was a painful stab. "Please don't, Dad. Not yet, please. War's almost over. I'll be home soon. Please wait."

"Okay, son. You're going to stay in the Consular Service, aren't you?"

"I don't think so!"

He heard the disappointment in his father's voice. "Hell of a fine calling, the Foreign Service, and one day you'll–"

"Dad, I'll talk to you all about that soon." He glanced at his watch. "I'll write you about it. You caught me at a very bad time; I'm up to my neck in something. Gotta go, lots of love, call you tomorrow."

He hung up and left the room.

He went downstairs and got into the waiting Consular car. They drove down tree-lined Paseo de las Delicias, along the Guadalquivir, until they came to the building with an American flag flying over its arched doorway. Built for the 1929's World's Fair, it was one of America's handsomest foreign-based buildings, both an office and a residence for the Consul, standing alone in a wedge of lush garden adjacent to María Luisa Park.

Wilson jumped out of the car before it stopped. "Pepe, be back here at five-thirty exactly."

The chauffeur's brow wrinkled as he said: "*Señor,* I cannot. I must take Señor Consul and his *esposa* to the function for Generalíssimo Franco."

Mierda. He'd forgotten there was a big diplomatic do

for Franco in the lavish reception pavilion in the park. Wilson was expected to attend also, along with all the Consular corps of Sevilla and the rich bigwigs, like Medinacelli and the Duchess of Alba and Doña Sol and famous General Queipo de Llano – a command performance. He could still put in an appearance at the end of it, after seeing that the German got his passport and freed Mia.

"All right, Pepe," he said to the chauffeur. "See you *mañana*."

An old doorman opened the iron gates and Wilson went into the office. Everything looked the way it had for the six months he'd been assigned there, even though the imminent prospect of the European war's end had changed the staff's attitudes in various degrees.

Moriarity, American clerk, twenty years in five countries, was at his desk, leafing through passport documentation. His shiny black suit caught sun filtering through an ornately grilled window. He was only semi-drunk.

The Spaniard, Gamarra, tight-lipped, slick-haired, pompous, was inordinately proud of having risen from office boy to his position in charge of bills of lading for Andalucia's exports to America. "Three-quarters of the world's sherry goes through me," was his little joke. The other quarter, it seemed to Wilson, went through Moriarity, and that was no joke.

Esperanza, a spinster secretary from the Canary Islands with a perennial look of disquietude, was busy sharpening pencils.

Old Marcos, porcine, was riffling through citizenship

applications, half asleep after a five-course luncheon.

The cute American secretary from Front Royal, Virginia, stood at the filing cabinets and winked at Wilson as he walked through the desks. Adelaide Fairchild winked at everyone. Like a tic, it was probably to avoid smiling, which showed her bad teeth. She always dressed in what looked like the flag of a Central American country, although Tottle regularly urged her to "dress more conservatively."

Wilson made his way to his desk next to Moriarity's. A small sign on Moriarity's desk read: *"Only Robinson Crusoe got his work done by Friday."* Consul Tottle had suggested once to Moriarity that the sign, "while mildly amusing," was hardly State Department issue and should be removed. Moriarity had said, "We'll see about that," but the sign remained. Nobody suggested much to Moriarity. Here was the engine room of this ship of fools they called the Consulate.

"Welcome back to the orifice," growled Moriarity. He had a perpetually morose expression. His shock of black hair was gray on the sides, and a lock of it hung on his forehead, down to his right eye. A jutting jaw always clenched the stem of an unlit pipe. Moriarity, irreverent and caustic, turned most people off. There existed a mystery about the man. Highly intelligent and superb at his job in spite of his alcoholic intake, he had remained a clerk all these years. Some assumed it was his daffy French wife's fault. Others suggested something "untoward" had happened at his last post, Berlin. Consul Tottle referred to it once as

"Moriarity's German incident."

Wilson liked him, appreciated his dry wit, cynicism, and independence, and felt awkward that he, at twenty-three, was a Vice Consul and Moriarity, at forty-five, was still a clerk. The hierarchy went like this: If Tottle was the general, Wilson was first lieutenant, Moriarity was a sergeant, and the Spanish clerks were privates. Wilson also liked the gentle, loving way Moriarity treated Colette, his wife. She was beautiful but always appeared to be in another world, one she saw through nervous and frightened eyes. "Positively certifiable" was the unfeeling way that Consul Tottle once put it.

"His Royal Highness requests an audience," Moriarity said, focusing bloodshot eyes upon Wilson. "As Escoffier might have inquired, how was lunch?"

"Mario's," Wilson answered, sitting down. "Instant trichinosis."

He stifled the urge to confide in Moriarity what was burning inside him; he alone might know how to handle the predicament. But what would he do? Alert the O.S.S. in Madrid, and then–? They were hundreds of miles away. Some immediate action was needed. But what alternatives were there at this point? The only thing to be done was to try to get the German his damned passport quickly, free Mia and the child, and then devise some plan of action.

"I've decided that our boss is the true Hobbesian man," said Moriarity. "He's nasty, he's brutish, and he's short. Otherwise, he's okay."

On Wilson's desk, next to his unfinished report on

"Franco's Post-War Plans for Spain," the secretary had placed three passports. He leafed through them quickly – one Congresswoman and two young Spaniards with dual citizenship. No good. He could see several passports on Moriarity's desk, but he didn't dare tell him, couldn't take the chance until Mia was free.

There was a small jar of paste on the desk, which he moved to his coat pocket. There was a letter from his mother. He picked up the letter opener and started to slit the envelope.

"You'd better get in there," said Moriarity. Born in Boston, he'd never even been to Ireland, yet there was that hint of a brogue that came and went. "Vlad the Impaler's a wee bit agitated."

Suddenly, Wilson decided. He would tell Frank the terrible problem; he had to.

"Frank," he said. "Listen to me. Mia, you know Mia, well, she…"

He got no further. The secretary stood in front of him.

"Mr. Tottle insists that you come in right now."

Wilson sighed and stood up. "Later," he said to Moriarity, then walked back to the Consul's office. "I'm back, sir."

Caleb Tottle was standing by the large map of Spain, talking on the phone in English, his only language after thirty-two years in foreign countries in the Consular Corps. A slim, dapper man dressed impeccably by the best London had to offer, he was always pleased to tell anyone his suits came from Poole's ("Mitchell's the best cutter in the world"), his shirts from New and Lingwood, his hats from Locke, and his well-boned shoes, which had never known a shoe-treeless night, over from Maxwell's by diplomatic courier. It was rumored that he had his suit pockets sewn shut so that he couldn't inadvertently put something in them to spoil the line.

"Ah, there you are, Tripp," the Consul said as he hung up. Tottle had a guardsman's mustache and talked as though it also grew inside his lip. "That was Sarlac from San Sebastian. Sounds as though it should spell something backwards, but it doesn't. He's all in a flap. Donovan's called also, from O.S.S."

Though originally from a rural town of 1,200 people in Nebraska, Tottle had managed to acquire an admirable international veneer and accent.

"The chaps in charge of rounding up the Nazis for trial are eager to get going – jump the gun if necessary – so that the bounders don't go underground. You and I should be prepared to take over the German Consulate in the next few days, whenever the surrender is completed. Meanwhile, Madrid says be on the lookout for any stray Nazis sneaking over from France." He paused, turned dramatically, and said in a lowered voice: "Day before yesterday. An old peasant killed in St. Pierre, France. Stripped. Then yesterday they found a dead fisherman near Irún. Stripped. Who'd kill a fisherman and strip him of his clothes?"

Wilson saw that the big safe in a corner of the room was partially open. Wilson made his voice dumb:

"Another fisherman?"

Tottle glared at him. "Oh-yes-of-course! And killed him with a German bullet probably fired from a Lüger! Obviously, it was someone trying to get into Spain in disguise."

Wilson moved casually over two steps so that he could see into the safe. On top of a codebook was the silver embosser, the official seal of the State Department.

"But Irún is a long way from us."

Consul Tottle turned to the map.

"Maybe heading for a rendezvous with a U-boat off of La Coruña." He jabbed a finger at the northern city, then corrected himself. "Portugal? I doubt it – another border to cross." He ran his manicured nail diagonally down Spain to Sevilla. "But since he knows they'll be looking for him up there, it would be smarter to hop a couple of freight trains, get here, and then go down to either this port" – his finger moved left to Huelva – "or over here," he pointed to Cadiz, to the right. "In either case, he could then nip over to Tangier or get out to a U-boat, or board a neutral ship going to South America, and it would be *adiós* to Mr. Kraut."

Tottle may have been a bit of a caricature, but he knew his geography, not only of Spain but the world. And besides being a first-class bridge player, he had some talent. He was proud of having been a star in the Hasty Pudding at Harvard, he played a pretty good jazz piano, and he did woodworking. But, as Moriarity said, "His main talent was being a pain in the ass."

Wilson barely trusted his voice to ask: "Who – who do

they think he is? Some big shot?"

Tottle answered: "Could be one of the biggest shots of all, Hitler's right arm – Martin Bormann."

"I heard on the radio that Bormann was killed outside of Hitler's bunker."

"Never know, probably was," said Tottle. "Those people in O.S.S. are so full of" – he caught himself – "poppycock."

"What do they say the man looks like?"

"Bormann?" Tottle said, picking up a sheet of paper from his desk. "Bormann, Martin. Five-foot-ten, husky, very strong, mustache, pale blue eyes, brown hair, meticulously dressed, likes shoes, left-handed, born in Halberstadt, Germany, 1900, came to power in meteoric rise in 1942, and so on. Who really gives a damn, he's not here in Spain, he's long gone."

"What would we do if we should happen to locate him?"

Tottle grunted. "We'd call Donovan and dump it in O.S.S.'s lap, that's what we'd do. Can't expect us to capture dangerous Nazis with fountain pens, now can they?"

"We wouldn't bring in the Spanish officials?"

"Hell, no! They'd give him a one-way ticket to Buenos Aires and a medal from Hitler's pal Franco! And speaking of Hitler, tell your little Nazi friend that if she hears of any undocumented Germans floating around, she can let us know and make some points. Might help her when she goes to trial."

"Sir, she is not a Nazi."

"Well, that remains to be seen, doesn't it?"

"I can swear to it."

"*Can* you? Proof? Evidence that she hasn't been mas-terminding getting the oil to the U-boats – our good American oil, intended solely to keep the Spaniards neu-tral – out to the submarines in fishing boats?"

"I will have proof for you," said Wilson. "Tomorrow I'll have proof, I promise you."

"Why are you so interested in her welfare, Tripp? You're not compromising yourself, are you?"

"No, sir. I just feel that…"

"Not getting a little Prussian stuff there, are you?"

Wilson felt his face flush; it was a strange choice of phrase, considering the Consul himself was married to a German woman.

The Consul opened a desk drawer and took out a deck of cards. "Got a new one for you, Wilson."

He only called Tripp by his first name before he per-formed his magic; while doing a trick he seemed more human, less of a caricature. "Okay," he said eagerly, "name a card, any card."

"Uh, the – the ten of spades, sir."

With deft fingers, the Consul began fanning out the cards, all face up.

"Your card, watch, will be the only one to be facing down."

Halfway through the deck a face-down card appeared.

"Turn it over," the Consul commanded confidently.

It was the ten of spades.

"Incredible," said Wilson. "How does it work – trick pack?"

Flushed with pride, the Consul chortled: "Oh, no, no trick packs here! I'll not reveal my secrets. You know something, I made money at Harvard with my magic act. First thing you learn: never divulge! Should have gone into it professionally."

Wilson edged over toward the safe. The embosser was sitting there, shining silver, ripe for the grabbing. If he could only distract Tottle long enough.

"Sir, I'd give anything to know how you do that trick," said Wilson, buying time. "I loved magic when I was a boy."

"Well," Tottle hesitated. "I shouldn't. But if you keep it to yourself." He held up the cards. "Ordinary deck, see? But on one side I've got all the even cards face up and" – he turned the deck over – "on this side all the odd ones face up. Each pair of cards adds up to thirteen, hearts with spades, clubs with diamonds. To find your ten of spades, all I had to do was fan out the cards until I came to the three of hearts – and I knew the ten was upside down behind it. Then I just–"

Before he could finish, the American secretary came to the door.

"Mr. Tottle, there's a Moses Byrd to see you." One eye winked automatically at anyone.

The Consul stroked his mustache with his forefinger. "Byrd? Moses Byrd?"

"Yes, sir. A colored gentleman."

"Oh, him." Tottle frowned. "Lord, what a nuisance. Well, I'd better get rid of blackie. Come along, Tripp."

The Consul and the secretary walked out the door.

Wilson went quickly to the safe, scooped up the embosser, squeezed it into his trouser pocket, and followed the Consul out through the main office. At the counter for the public was a thin black man dressed in a neat, worn, camel's-hair overcoat and an ancient homburg. He rested a silver-headed cane on his shoulder, and he wore shoes of cracked patent leather with bows.

The Consul approached him. "What can I do for you, George?"

"Moses, sir," the man corrected, gently but firmly. His speech was deeply Southern but well enunciated. "I am very desirous of returning to the States, sir."

"And you don't have money for a ticket, right?"

"That is correct, sir." He took off his hat and ran his hand over his white hair. "I do not have the fare."

"How long have you been in Spain, sport?"

"Let me see now." The man rolled his eyes ceilingward as he calculated. "Yessir, more than fifteen years, must be all of that. Stranded here back in twenty-nine, when the troupe I headed ran out of money."

"Troupe?" Wilson said. The embosser felt large and conspicuous in his pocket. Government property, stolen U.S. Government property, the precious guarded seal that some people would have, and had, killed for.

"Dance," the old man said with pride. "The Black an' Blues, we was called. Before Spain, we were in Paris, the opening act for the Ebony Venus, Josie Baker–"

"A dancer?"

"Yessir, tap and eccentric." He held out the heavy silver

head of his cane proudly. "See that there? Alfonso the Thirteenth! He give it to me personally after I performed for him once. That there's the Royal Seal."

A strange look came over the Consul's face. "Can you do this, Moses?"

To Wilson's astonishment, the Consul suddenly put his arms out from his side and did an intricate tap step with surprising agility. He ended with a "hah!", one knee bent and his right arm extended, seeking applause from an invisible audience.

"Hasty Pudding, Harvard," he panted, flushed with pride. "Can you do that?"

"No, sir," said Byrd solemnly. "I don't believe I could do that there one."

"I'll teach it to you one of these days," said Tottle, straightening his tie.

"In the words of the great Fats Waller, sir, one never knows, do one."

"Can you still dance, Moses?"

"A little, sir."

"We might hire you for one of our parties. Let's see you in action."

The black man shook his head. "Been a long time, sir. Gettin' old…"

"Come on, just a step or two."

"Here in this office – and without music?"

"Come on, George," the Consul prodded. "Maybe here's a way to make a little money for your fare to the States. People at the party might hire you, too."

The man hesitated. Then he took off his coat and carefully draped it on the counter. He squared his shoulders. He took the cane and planted it elegantly, almost delicately, on the floor with one hand. Raising the other hand, he began to snap his fingers with a crack. A soft melodic hum came from his lips, and the eyes went closed as a little smile came to one corner of his mouth. He stood more erect and seemed to grow younger before their eyes.

"Doo dah, doo dah," Byrd murmured. "Yeah!" He looked down at the cane as though it were some kind of a magic wand. Slowly, he began to move around it, feet sliding in an intricate pattern, soles of his patent leather shoes never leaving the floor, right hand moving rhythmically as though throwing dice and cracking out the beat. He slithered his way completely around the cane. Then he suddenly yanked up the stick, twirled it like a cheerleader's baton, and both feet burst into a machine gun volley. He tapped up to the counter, backed five feet away, then circled, still tapping in an ever-increasing staccato. As the rat-a-tat-tat crescendoed, he leapt into the air, came down in the splits, oozed himself up to his feet and made an elegant bow, his brown face glowing and glistening with sweat.

The office personnel clapped in delighted surprise, and the Consul said: "Not bad, not bad at all, Mr. Byrd, really great. Tell you what, Moses, you teach me that, and I'll show you some great magic tricks."

"Sounds good to me," Moses panted.

"Back to business," said Tottle. "So, suddenly after

twenty years, Mr. Byrd, you want to go back to your beloved America. Why the rush?"

"Well, sir, war's almost over, and my wife – she was Spanish–" he swallowed twice. "She died last week." He cleared his throat. "Spent my last *peseta* on her funeral. I'm not getting any younger, sir, and when my time comes I want to be home. I still got people in Virginia, and I want to die and be buried in them beautiful hills."

"Mr. Byrd, I appreciate that sentiment, and I admire you people, always have. But you must understand that we're not a charitable institution. We just don't have the funds for such things."

Wilson thought of the seven-hundred-dollar cocktail reception the Consulate had given a week ago for the Baroness of La Huerta, whose sole distinction was that she'd once been named in *Vogue* magazine one of the world's best-dressed women and was a friend of the Consul's wife.

The black man frowned. "But, sir, if I was to die here in Spain, you would then ship my body home, would you not? How come you can't ship that same old body home when it's still alive?"

"I'm sorry, sport," Tottle said, putting his hand on the black man's shoulder. "I'm afraid we can't do anything for you."

The old man was breathing hard now, and his voice was husky. With a long finger he pointed out the window at the river.

"Sir, if I could just get down to the big port of Cadiz, I know I could get a job on a ship, bussing dishes. Got friends in Cadiz, and I–"

"What's the real reason?"

"Sir?"

"Spaniards giving you a bad time? Because you're American? And colored? And we won the war?"

The man hesitated and then nodded. "Well, there's that. There is a bad element, sir, who are bedeviling me and certain other Americans. I got to get out for my life."

"I am truly sorry, Mr. Byrd. Afraid I can't help you."

The Consul started to turn away.

"Mr. Tottle," Wilson said, "don't we have an emergency fund?"

"Yes, we do," said the Consul, adding pointedly: "It's for emergencies."

The Consul walked away, calling back over his shoulder, "Don't forget General Franco this evening."

Wilson turned. "Mr. Byrd, I'm sorry. But give me your address."

The man wrote on a piece of paper and handed it to Wilson. As he put it in his pocket, Wilson noticed that the address was very near Mia's. "I'll do my best," he said.

Moses Byrd gave a sad smile as he put on his overcoat. "I do believe you will, sir, and I thank you."

He shuffled out of the door, and Wilson walked back to his desk, glancing at the clock.

Jesus. Five-fifteen and no passport. Moriarity wasn't at his desk. In the "Out" basket was a pile of green American passports, Moriarity being the resident visa expert. He was undoubtedly in the bathroom, not relieving himself, but having the hourly slug of Fundador or Irish whiskey, what he called his "obligatory face tighteners," from the curved silver flask he carried in his pocket.

"I was born two drinks under par," he liked to say. Often.

Wilson eased over to the desk and riffled through the passports, turning quickly to the photo page of each. Finally he came to a businessman from Wilton, Connecticut, one Seymour A. Boyd, aged fifty-five. Too old, but it said he had blue eyes. It would have to do. He carefully slipped the passport into his pocket and rearranged the others.

"Help you?" said Moriarity behind him. Wilson could smell the brandy through the mint.

Wilson turned. "Thought you might have taken one of my citizenship cases."

"Now why would I be doing a thing like that, bucko?" Moriarity's eyes were sparkling. Had he seen him take the passport, or was it just the liquor?

Wilson lowered his voice. "Listen, Frank, I need your help, badly."

Moriarity sat at his desk. "I am known as a friend to the downtrodden and weak and needy of this world. Shoot."

"Seriously, Frank. This is important! I've got to talk to you!"

"Talk away." He leafed through the passports idly. "As Mrs. Christopher Columbus, wife of the Genovese explorer, used to say, 'press on, laddie, press on.'"

"No, wait." Wilson looked at his watch. "Forget it. I've got to go. Late. I'll meet you at seven exactly."

"Can't. Franco's shindig."

"Frank, this may be the biggest thing you've ever done in your whole life."

"That wouldn't be saying much, bucko," Moriarity said quietly. But he saw the urgency and desperation in Wilson's face. "Where?"

Wilson thought a second. "The little bar near the bridge. You know, near the boats."

"On the Triana side?"

"La Querencia, I think it's called."

Moriarity nodded. "Know it well." Then, as Wilson turned to leave, he said: "Oh, and laddie, you *will* bring the passport back when you've quite done with it, won't you? It belongs to one of the largest importers of sherry in America."

Wilson felt his face color. But he didn't answer and went out of the Consulate fast.

He saw the first one fold a newspaper as he passed the cathedral. Then they were three, all with newspapers under their elbows. Not very subtle; he crossed the square, they crossed the square, he went down a side street, they went down a side street. They'd probably been following him since he left the Consulate.

He watched them in the glass of a store's show window as they crossed Almendro Street. One small man in front, two larger thugs on either side, all three dressed in dark suits and ties, the middle one bareheaded, the others wearing berets. The leader looked familiar; he'd seen that mean, pinched face before. Where?

He glanced at his watch. Twelve minutes to make the German's deadline. Mia's apartment was only two hundred yards away, but now he couldn't go directly to it, not with these goons, whoever they were, following him; the German would be looking out the window and might assume the men were with Wilson and kill his hostages.

Wilson walked down a cobbled street that would take him behind Mia's apartment. From there, he could double around. Out of sight of his pursuers, he broke into a limping trot down the deserted street. He remembered where he'd seen the little one before. Several months ago, the Consulate had received a tip from the O.S.S. that a huge shipment of "oranges" was on a train headed for Germany via France and that the crates contained wolfram, vital to the manufacture of steel. Moriarity and Wilson, with two Spanish policemen, had found the freight cars in the Jaen train yards at midnight. They had impounded the cargo. The sender was heavily fined, blacklisted, and virtually ruined. The man's name was López, and at his hearing he had sworn revenge on the American Consulate in general and the Vice Consul in particular.

It hadn't worried Wilson at the time. Now was another story. The delay it might cause. He glanced at his watch as he walked. Close, because of the detour, but all right. Then, out of a narrow alley, the three men appeared in front of him.

"Ah hah, Señor Vice Consul!" said López. The mouth was stretched into a semblance of a smile beneath the pencil mustache. The oiled black hair was parted in the middle. "We meet again."

Natty in a white shirt and silver tie, López stood in front of the other two, feet apart, hands in his pockets, not one to be mussed himself. One of the men had a knife in his hand and the other was snapping open his blade. Wilson was taken aback by this, not so much by the potential danger, but by the openness. It was broad daylight, a main street, anyone could walk by. He crouched slightly, his good leg forward.

"I will not kill you, *señor*, the way you and your people have killed the greatest regime of all history, the Third Reich. I will not kill you as you deserve, for having caused my ruination. You will merely bear a swastika on your forehead for life so as to better remember me and these happy times."

If you'd mind waiting a few moments, I'll take down my pants, extract my trusty Army knife from my brace, and we'll match blade for blade.

Then, with both hands, López motioned for the two men to step forward, but before they could, Wilson leapt at López. One hand caught the little man by the throat, the other reached out and clutched his crotch. López screamed as Wilson lifted him up, yanked him back, and then raked the man's body across his companions as they lunged forward. All three went down on the cobblestones. *Not bad for a gimp*, thought Wilson as he turned and ran. He went swerved up the first side alley he came to, hoping it would lead to the street where Mia lived.

Then he saw that it was a dead end. He heard footsteps slapping the cobblestones as the men rounded the corner. Only the two with the knives now. They were sixty feet away. There were several doorways, and Wilson pounded on one thick door.

"*Socorro*," he yelled. "Help, please!"

He pounded on another and another. As they bore down on him, he slid into a corner, his back against the wall, ready to use his feet.

One man was in the lead, his knife hand extended. When he was practically upon him, Wilson lunged forward, whirled and lashed out with his right leg. He caught the man solidly in the ribs, and the Spaniard collapsed with a groan. Wilson caught the other man by the wrist and twisted it until the knife clattered to the cobblestones. But the man staggered back and fumbled inside his coat. He withdrew a small pistol and raised it.

Suddenly, from an alleyway, a dark figure appeared behind the man. There was a loud crack, and Wilson watched in disbelief as the gunman sagged to the ground.

Wilson saw a dark-skinned man standing over the crumpled body. Then he recognized the silver-headed cane held by Moses Byrd.

"Quick, sir!" said Byrd, taking Wilson by the arm. He pulled him down the street. "Other fellow be right along now."

They came to an open doorway and Moses shoved

Wilson into it. He fell hard on a carpeted floor. He heard the door clang shut and the bolt being thrown. He was helped to his feet. His eyes grew accustomed to the gloom.

"Thank you," Wilson breathed. "Where the hell did you come from?"

"Providence," said the man simply. "Actually, I live here. I happened to be watching them. They followed you; I followed them. They been after me, too, for being American and colored."

"Got to get out of here."

"They gonna wait on you it takes all night. Got a back way."

He turned and went through the long basement apartment. Following, Wilson made out a large photograph of Roosevelt and another of a pretty Spanish woman in a dancer's costume. A faded poster proclaimed: "The Great Colored American Dance Troupe, The Black an' Blues In An All-Star Revue!"

They came to a small window, and Moses unbolted the grill and yanked it open. He pulled a chair over below it.

"You'll come out on Flores Street."

Wilson shook his head. "They're going to lay for you now."

"I be all right."

"You meant it about Cadiz? Once there you could get a boat to the States?"

"Yessir, if I could just get to Cadiz, I got friends there."

"Could you go tonight, now?"

Moses nodded. "Sure thing."

Wilson took out his wallet and extracted a hundred-dollar bill, his last money till payday.

"Here's the fare," he said, shoving it in the man's hand. "The *Cayetana* leaves at seven. Triana Pier!"

Moses stared at the money. "God bless you, man."

Wilson got up on the chair and wriggled through the window and sprawled down on the sidewalk. He got up and looked at his watch. He sprinted to Mia's apartment and jabbed the doorbell twice. The door opened a crack. The German looked out over Wilson's head, then opened the door wider, and Wilson stepped in.

"Six minutes ahead of time," Wilson said, panting. "Let her go!"

"We talk first," said the German.

The pistol, with silencer attached, was in his left hand. He looked completely different. He had shaved and bathed, the mustache was gone, and he was dressed in a tie and a gray flannel suit, appropriated from Mia's husband's closet. His shoes were shined, and he now could very well pass for an American businessman.

Wilson handed the passport, the embosser, and the paste jar to the German, who went to the sofa and sat down, putting the pistol and the other objects in front of him.

"Ah hah," he said as he leafed through the passport. "How do you do, Mister Seymour Boyd of Connecticut?" When he pronounced the second "c" in the name of the state as in "connection," Wilson didn't correct him; it might help trip him up somewhere along the line.

"Where's Mia?" Wilson watched the man remove a photo from his pocket.

"She went to the store," said the man, carefully peeling off the photo inside the passport.

"You let her *go*?" Wilson exclaimed incredulously.

"To get some food for the daughter for the trip. She looked weak."

"You let her go free?"

"Mister Tripp, one can see my goddaughter is very fond of you. She would not endanger your life by running away. She will meet us at the boat in just a short time now."

"Us?" Wilson asked.

"My dear fellow–" the German coated the back of his photo with the little brush attached to the jar's lid. "A sea change will do you good. You are an American official and you speak Spanish. I need you."

Wilson sagged. Of course, he should have known that the bastard wouldn't – couldn't – leave him behind.

"Once in Cadiz, you are free."

"And Mia and her daughter?" he asked. "They go free also?"

The German frowned. "Of course."

He pressed the photograph down on the passport, then slid the page into the embosser, squeezing down on the handle until the seal of the United States was raised in little bumps across his likeness. He held up the passport and admired his work. "If the authorities don't look too closely at Mr. Seymour Boyd, they will–"

When the doorbell rang, the German glared at Wilson. "You told someone!"

"I swear!" said Wilson.

The German snatched up the pistol. He strode to the window and looked through the Venetian blinds. He came back and put on a gabardine raincoat, which had been draped over a chair. The large pocket swallowed the pistol and its attachment.

The bell sounded again. He put on the plaid canvas hat, and then with a look that warned Wilson of potential mayhem if he said anything, the German opened the door.

"Hello, *madame*," he said cheerily, "Just on my way out. Help you?"

She stood there – a woman of about twenty-two or -three, dark glasses with heavy black rims and black hair pulled back in a bun, its blackness interrupted by a white streak on the left side; the only time Wilson had seen hair like that was on the *matador* Manolete. Very striking. She wore a cashmere sweater over a starched white shirt, a plaid skirt, flat shoes, and she carried a large no-nonsense purse. Wilson had seen her before. When she spoke he knew where.

"Mia, I say, is she all right?"

He knew from the voice and the accent that she was from the British Consulate, Nigel Burke's secretary. They'd met once at some official function. Gilly something.

She was not unattractive, actually quite handsome, but he had found her *teddibly* Brit, aloof, uncommunicative, and almost rude, all in the space of their five-minute non-relationship. He'd made a bad *gaffe* at the start; when she'd remarked that she got "a good screw each month," he'd come back with: "That's a lot better than I'm doing!" Later he learned that the English called a salary "a screw," and he felt very foolish.

"She is fine," said the German. "Gone out. Now, if you will excuse me–"

"She certainly didn't sound fine on the phone," said the woman curtly. "Who are you?"

"I am her godfather, and if you don't mind I am–"

"Oh, hello," said the woman as she saw Wilson. "You're the American Vice Consul." She pushed by the German, into the room.

"Gilly Leigh-Jones," she said in her cool, controlled voice. "Damn strange, that call. Where is she?"

"Apparently went to the store with her daughter," said Wilson.

"Didn't sound like that to me on the phone," said the woman.

"We go now to meet with her," said the German with a smile. "We are in a big hurry, that is why I do not offer tea. I know how you English like your tea, Miss Jones."

Wilson saw that the German could make himself very charming when he wanted to. And he also saw that any charm was lost on the Englishwoman.

"*Leigh*-Jones," she corrected sharply. "You're sure she's not here? She sounded ill or frightened."

His smile faded. "Quite sure, dear *madame*." He

turned to Wilson. "We leave *now.*"

Wilson stalled for time. "You're a friend of Mia's?"

"Yes. She did such an extraordinarily nice thing. When she heard my parents had been killed in London two months ago, she rang up to commiserate. Hers were killed also. Dresden."

"And she called just now?" asked Wilson.

"We go, Mr. Tripp." The German tapped his watch.

"About twenty minutes ago. Just a couple of words I couldn't understand, then a strange sound, and the voice broke off. Bloody odd."

The German took Wilson by the arm in a steely grip. "You must excuse us, dear *madame.*"

There was a noise, a dog's scratching, and it came from behind the closed bedroom door.

"Come," the German said, guiding Wilson to the door forcefully. "We go!"

"Poor Schatzi's locked in," said Gilly, starting for the door.

"Stop!" ordered the German. "Do not go there!"

But she was already at the door and opening it.

"Come away!" shouted the German.

Schatzi came out, whining as the door opened.

"I told you to stop." The German drew his pistol from his raincoat slowly, almost reluctantly. "I am sorry you did not heed me."

Inside the room Wilson and the woman saw an open suitcase on the bed and beside it the lifeless form of the girl, a bullet hole in the center of her forehead. Mia lay on the floor in a fetal position, her face covered with blood.

"I told you to stop," muttered the German, shaking his head as he cocked the pistol. "Foolish, foolish English girl."

4

Wilson gave a bellow of rage and leapt at the German, but his hooked fingers never reached the man's throat. There was the flash of the pistol, and dimly he felt the barrel smash into the side of his forehead, before he crumpled to the floor.

He lay there not totally unconscious, merely stunned by the expert blow. Above him, he could hear the voices, quite far away, as though in another room. The first was Gilly Leigh-Jones's cry. Then a moan, and then her steely: "You bloody monster!"

"*Madame,* watch your tongue," he heard the German say, "or you will join them. Sit! Over there!"

The dog howled once.

"Be quiet, Schatzi. Do not make me kill you."

The dog howled again.

Wilson heard the refrigerator door open. Then: "Here, Schatzi, good meat. Be quiet now, good dog."

Wilson heard the kitchen faucet running and a glass being filled. Then the footsteps approached, and he felt the water splash down on his face.

"Get up!" The command seemed to come from far away.

Wilson shook his head to clear it. More water.

"Get up! You are not hurt."

Slowly, Wilson pulled himself up and stood, swaying slightly, his fingers to his head. He stared at the bedroom. The door was closed now.

"You fucking Kraut," Wilson growled. "I will kill you for this, you know that."

"What is this with the Kraut?" the man said lightly. "I am an American, an importer of sherry, Mister Seymour Boyd. And this" – he put his arm and the hand holding the pistol around the English girl – "is my darling wife."

Shrinking from him, Gilly whispered: "Monster!"

"No." The German looked at his watch. "No, my dear, I am no monster. I have a beloved wife named Gerda in Germany I would like to see again. I have children I love. I have a dear dog like Schatzi. In fact, I raise Schatzies. I am no monster. I am merely a patriot who does what must be done. She," – he jerked his head toward the bedroom – "I caught her phoning the English Consulate, calling this woman here, and the little girl was screaming, so I did what I had to do, only what I was forced to do. I did not like to do it, I hated to do it, but I must get to the boat. This is far more important than just my life. Or yours. Sometime you will find out how important, perhaps." He glanced at his watch again. "We will be right on time. Come, we go now."

He looked out of the window, then went to the door. He unscrewed the silencer, put it in one pocket of his raincoat, then put the pistol in the other. He kept his left hand on the pistol. He opened the door and motioned for Wilson to go first. When Wilson hesitated, the German jabbed the pistol into his hip. Gilly followed Wilson. The German closed the door behind them.

"Walk," he commanded, "toward the river."

They went down the sidewalk, Gilly and Wilson, still shaky from the blow, in front, the German very close behind. The street was bustling; Spain stays light until late, and the cities come to life after the long afternoon *siesta*.

"We are a happy family," said the German under his breath. "We are out for a stroll, a very pleasant little stroll."

At the end of the block, they could see several parked horse-drawn carriages, still the principal form of taxi in Sevilla.

"When we get there," the German ordered Wilson, "engage a cab to go to the boat. Do not try warning the cabbie in Spanish. I will know, and the woman will die first. Then you."

Moriarity, thought Wilson. Moriarity would be at La Querencia Cafe. Somehow he might be able to do something. It was the only hope. Otherwise, what did he have? A knife – a little larger than a Boy Scout's. And it was clear that no matter what the German said he would be obliged to kill Gilly and himself, either during or at the end of this trip.

5

Klaus Stryker, the German Vice Consul, was in his small apartment only four blocks away from where Mia lived, packing a suitcase, when there came a loud knocking on his door.

"*Quien es?*" the big man asked warily.

A reply came in steely German. "Open up, Stryker."

He opened the door but kept the chain on. He was looking into a face whose pale green eyes, below a black hat, were almost as cold as his own. He took a pistol from the holster under his arm. "Yes?"

"Open the door!" It was a voice not used to being disobeyed, whose accent was pure Berlin.

"What do you want?"

"Important," said the stranger, then added, "it is

important for you, Herr Stryker."

Stryker hesitated.

"Open!" commanded the man.

The Vice Consul slid the bolt back and cautiously opened the door. A man in a shiny black leather coat and black fedora stepped inside and slammed the door behind him. "Put the pistol away, Herr Vice Consul," he said quietly. "You stupid son of a bitch."

"Who are you?" Stryker demanded. "What do you want?"

"Who I am doesn't matter," said the man in black. "What I want does. Put the pistol away."

When Stryker complied, the man noted the open, half-filled suitcase on the bed. "You were going someplace?"

"The Consulate is no more. The Third Reich is no more. I am going to Paris."

"No. You are going to South America."

"I have a woman," said Stryker. "In Paris."

"Listen, Herr Vice Consul," the man said. "You will be a hero. We are giving you the greatest assignment of your life. You should be grateful."

"I'm going to Paris."

"A very important personage has arrived today with us, by a most circuitous route. It has been a dangerous enterprise, but we have succeeded in getting him this far. I can go no further. We can't risk failure. You have a diplomatic passport. You can get him to his destination."

"Which is?"

"The end of the river."

"Cadiz?"

"Near there. You will escort him with your life."

"Who is this – this personage?" Stryker sneered. "The Führer?"

"One might say," said the man calmly, "at this particular time, that he could be considered more important than the Führer. Much, much more important."

"Himmler?" said Stryker. "Goering? Hess?"

"Don't be ridiculous. Those clowns are already in the hands of the Americans. They will be hanged."

Stryker shook his head and ran his hand over his blond crew cut. "I am not going to cooperate."

"You have no choice," said the man. "You are going to get on a boat" – he removed a piece of paper from the pocket of his raincoat and glanced at it – "called the *Cayetana*. Be at the Triana dock at seven o'clock tonight. There will be other people on board, including a fellow German of some prominence whom you will recognize. You will proceed down the river to the meeting place. You will get aboard a vessel, and you will stay with your *responsibility* until he and you are safely in Argentina. Your client will be going on to Japan, but that is not your concern or your business. You will know nothing, which should come naturally to you. Your contact in Buenos Aires will see that you return to Germany or Paris or wherever you wish, to much money for a job well done."

"And if I refuse?"

The man in black took out a silver cigarette case. "Your real name is Wilhelm Muller Hickmann." He popped it open, extracted a cigarette, tapped it on the back of his left hand, put it in his mouth, and lit it with a gold lighter. "When you were fourteen, your stepfather was murdered, most probably by you. You joined Hitler Youth. You were briefly in the Gestapo. They didn't like you, for various reasons," his slight sneer suggesting those "various reasons" had to do with sexual preference. "You were ousted and transferred in 1943 to Auschwitz in Poland, assistant in command no less, where even there you made a reputation as, shall we say, too strict a disciplinarian. Eventually, the commandant asked for your dismissal. You then went to Munich." He clucked disapprovingly. "My, you seem to have such a terrible temper, Wilhelm, I mean Klaus. Among other events, you were linked to the murder of a pregnant woman, a married Swedish girl, but there was not enough evidence to convict you. You then totally changed your identity, that took talent, and somehow you talked your way into the Consular Corps and were sent here to Sevilla. Is that enough for you? I have more."

"What have those lies got to do with anything?" Stryker growled.

"Listen, Herr Vice Consul, you miserable piece of *sheit*," said the man. "The Americans are rounding up war criminals for trial. I'm sure they would be very interested in Vice Consul Klaus Stryker's true identity and whereabouts." He held out the silver case. "Cigarette?"

Stryker shook his head. He paced uncomfortably in the small room. "And where is your precious personage?"

The man went to the door and whistled. Another man appeared in the doorway accompanied by a very small figure, a little man in a gray trench coat, black beret, and dark glasses, who carried a briefcase that was handcuffed to his wrist. The man seemed familiar to Stryker, but it was hard to tell given the man's dark glasses and the turned-up raincoat collar.

"There is your client and assignment," said the man. "He has agreed that if there is any danger of his falling into the hands of the Americans, you are to shoot him and dispose of the briefcase in any way you can, even if you have to cut his hand off at the wrist. It must not under, any circumstances, come into the enemy's hands. You can see that he is a true patriot of the Third Reich. Is everything now clear and understood?"

The Vice Consul nodded numbly.

"*Sehr güt,*" the man in black said. "And one little piece of advice, Herr Hickmann, I would seriously consider, once in Argentina, staying there indefinitely." The man looked at his watch. "You have little time, Vice Consul. I can't tell you more now, but you will be a great hero if all goes well. If not–" he shrugged significantly. Then he raised his arm. "Heil, Hitler."

The three other men raised their arms and echoed, "Heil Hitler."

6

When Mia heard the apartment door close, she staggered up. She stumbled, sobbing and bloody, to the front window, peering out long enough to see the German, Gilly, and Wilson moving down the street, toward the cab stand.

When she returned to her daughter's lifeless body on the bed, she took one of the girl's hands in both of hers and held it against her bloody cheek.

"Liebchen, liebchen," she moaned, over and over. "Heidi, Heidi." The girl had been doomed, probably; Mia had steeled herself for her inevitable death from her illness, but not so soon, not this way!

She felt the blood running down her own neck and chest. Ignoring her wounds, she lurched into the bathroom, where she took a washcloth, soaked it in water from the basin, and returned to Heidi. Kneeling, she tenderly wiped away the blood from the wound in the ashen forehead. She turned the bloody pillow over and gently crossed the thin arms across the body. She put Heidi's beloved teddy bear on the pillow, beside her head.

"Sleep, darling, sleep," she murmured through sobs.

Then, abruptly, she straightened and stopped crying. She cleared her throat.

"Oh, that bastard, that bastard!"

Wiping the back of her fingers across her eyes, she stood and returned to the bathroom. She examined her bloody head in the mirror. She filled the basin with cold water and with a towel began cleaning herself. She parted the hair above her right ear and saw the raw crease the bullet had made; it had not caught the head full on since she'd had the telephone to her ear.

But the groove was deep, angry, and still bleeding. She held the wet towel against the wound while she opened the medicine cabinet and fumbled out a sanitary pad. Back in the bedroom, not allowing herself to look at the body on the bed, she yanked open the top drawer of the dresser and took out a scarf. She pressed the napkin against the wound and tied the scarf tightly around her head.

Taking off the bloody blouse and skirt, she thought for a moment, and then, in panties and bra, she went to the maid's closet beyond the kitchen. She snatched a black work dress from the hook and went back to the bedroom. After putting it on, she found a black shawl and drew it over her head. She looked at herself in the mirror. Fierce eyes stared back out of hollows at her, eyes dark with hatred.

She reached into the drawer beyond the scarves and her fingers closed around the little pistol, the .25-caliber Krüpp revolver her husband had given her for protection. Some protection it had been. But now she had another use for it. She put it in the pocket of the dress and left the apartment quickly.

7

Frank Moriarity, at his desk in the Consulate, looked at his watch. Twenty of seven. He'd better leave if he were to meet Tripp as promised in Triana. And what was this all about? Why the urgency and secrecy? And why did Wilson need to swipe one of the passports?

Frank Moriarity had no desire to meet General Francisco Franco – or any other Fascist, for that matter. He'd had his fill of them back in the Consulate in Germany, even before one of their future Nazi leaders raped his wife at a house party in the country near Munich. Not only did the man rape her, but he invited two of his drunken buddies to partake of her after him. His wife, his gorgeous petite French wife, had not been the same since. She seemed to live in another world now. Moriarity knew that other Foreign Service officers described her as "poor Colette. Quite nutsy, you know." He'd actually overheard the German bitch that Consul Tottle was married to refer to Colette once that way in her inimitable way of speaking; she hadn't known Moriarity was listening: "Not crazy, you realize, not really crazy, just a little fey. Poor Frank, no wonder he drinks."

Moriarity had never known that Nazi's name, but he'd seen him briefly when the German had picked up Colette at their hotel in Munich. He'd been driving a Mercedes limousine, with two other Nazi buckos in back. Moriarity had escorted her to the car, but he'd had to stay at the Consulate for an unexpected crisis; he was to join the party the next day. Instead, Colette was brought back to him early the next morning by the distressed hostess and host, who professed ignorance and shock at Colette's condition and story. Colette was hysterical and almost incoherent, bruised badly, her dress torn.

The ringleader, the driver of the car, had eyes that Moriarity would not forget. The rest of the face was vague, but he would never forget the eyes. According to Colette, the others called him Bootsie, but that was the only name she heard during the two-hour gang rape in the back of the limousine, parked on a side road near the country house. Colette spent three weeks in the sanitarium and seemingly was all right when she left. But Moriarity knew she would never be the same. He had tried to find out the Nazi's name, to kill him, but no one seemed to know anything. The host and hostess claimed, probably truthfully, that they had not invited any members of the Nazi party that weekend. The police did nothing. The man was obviously important, since he had been driven in an official Nazi limousine. It was rumored around the Consulate that he was a confidante of Adolf Hitler, who was fast coming to total power, but which confidante? No one had heard of a top Nazi with the nickname of Bootsie or Putzi. Moriarity, stonewalled at every turn, was making himself a nuisance with his constant inquiries. He was an embarrassment to the Foreign Service, which was doing its best to get along with this new Germany. Moriarity, drinking more and more, was passed over for promotion to Vice Consul, and he was abruptly assigned to Sevilla as soon as Colette was able to travel. The Moriaritys, in spite of his experience and expertise, were not considered any prize gift, and the Tottles distanced themselves from them.

Frank Moriarity had no love for Fascists, and this kowtowing to Franco tonight, to Hitler's buddy, was galling to him. Over at the pavilion in María Luisa Park, he would have to stand in line with the rest of the con-sular corps, British, French, German, whatever, to shake this little bastard's hand, or bow or salute or kiss his ass, or whatever one was supposed to do.

But first, he had to meet young Tripp and find out what was so damned urgent. Tripp was a nice guy, one of the few good Ivy Leaguers he'd met in the Foreign Service, and he must be in some kind of trouble from the look of it. Otherwise, why was he swiping passports on the sly? Moriarity was cutting the rendezvous time pretty close, but as it was, he was leaving work early. Vice Consuls could leave early. Clerks were supposed to stay until seven. He put the passports in a drawer and locked it. As he got up from his desk, Consul Tottle appeared in front of him.

"Mr. Moriarity, please come into my office."

Moriarity glanced at his watch and followed Tottle. As the Consul sat at his desk, Moriarity started: "I had a medical appointment downtown, sir, so I–"

"No matter." The Consul waved his hand and picked up a sheaf of papers. "Now, what do you know of this American *matador,* Sidney Phillips? Sit."

Reluctantly, Moriarity sat. "I've met him once or twice, sir. He's about forty, here in Spain to try a comeback. Over the hill, I'd say. Pleasant enough fellow, I guess, though a loudmouth."

"It says here that he was from Brooklyn, a confidante of Hemingway's during the Spanish Civil War. Had a fairly successful career as a *matador,* until a bull gored him."

"Where, sir?"

"Geographically, in Madrid," said Tottle. "Anatomically, in the rectum."

Moriarity essayed a quick smile. "Bulls will do that, I'm told. But sir, I really have to–"

Tottle went back to the dossier.

"Forty-three years old, has been living in Mexico and Texas, performing occasionally and without success. Has had numerous bullfighting protégés whom he introduces as his nephews."

Moriarity glanced at his watch and got up. "Sir, my appointment."

Tottle went on reading. "Came to Sevilla two years ago trying to get fights, opened up a little school for young bullfighters. Numerous complaints lodged against him of a sexual nature, pedophilia. None substantiated." Tottle closed the folder. "Now, Frank, I've just had a phone call from the Chief of Police. He says that Phillips has really done it this time. One of this *matador's* so-called disciples was the teenage son of a most distinguished man in this city, the Marqués de la Huerta. The Marqués claims that Phillips molested his son."

"You mean," said Moriarity, "he buggered him?"

Tottle nodded. "Repeatedly. The Marqués has vowed to shoot him on sight. The police are looking for him. Might have skipped town, or he might seek asylum here in the Consulate. Don't give it to him. Turn the fruit over to the police at once. The Marquesa is a good friend of my wife."

"I don't hold with rapists of any kind," said Moriarity. "But maybe the man is innocent."

"Stow the humanitarian sentiments, Moriarity," said Tottle. "Turn him over to the police. We want no part of that fruitcake." He took out his deck of cards from a drawer. "Frank, name a card, any card at all."

"Sorry!" Moriarity got up. "I'm late, sir, very late!"

"You're missing a great trick, Frank."

"Tomorrow, sir! Promise."

He left the office before the Consul could order him to stay. As he reached the front gate he heard an anguished cry.

"Poochie!"

He looked up to the second story of the Consulate and saw his wife framed in the bedroom window of their apartment. She was naked, and her once beautiful face was twisted with fear.

"Poochie, viens ici!" she cried. "I need you!"

"Colette, I can't! I'm late!"

"Poochie, come up!"

He looked at his watch in exasperation. "I can't, darling, I can't!"

"Help, Poochie," she yelled. "He is going to fawk me!"

"Oh, God," Moriarity said, and ran back into the Consulate.

8

The open horse carriage with its three passengers clopped across the bridge to Triana. Over the shoulders of Gilly and the German, Wilson could see the Querencia bar on the riverfront. A few patrons sat at the outside tables.

As the carriage drew closer, Wilson searched eagerly for any sign of Moriarity.

The carriage proceeded along the quay for a hundred yards, and when it came alongside the *Cayetana,* Wilson said: *"Aquí."*

The coachman reined up his horse.

"We get out now," said the German, teeth clenched and with a forced smile. "We are all very jolly, going for a nice little ride on the nice little boat." The pistol in his raincoat prodded Wilson's hip. "Smile, Mr. Vice Consul."

Wilson widened his mouth and stepped down from the carriage, followed by Gilly and the German, who handed the coachman some money. The carriage clattered away.

The *Cayetana* rocked slightly at its mooring. Nacho, the captain, was helping an old woman down from the gangplank to the deck. Wilson recognized her as Miss Gold, first name unknown to most of the world but not to Wilson, who'd seen her passport; her name was Esmeralda, and she was seventy-eight years old. She was an American historian who had spent over forty years in Sevilla, studying the Columbus voyages in the Archives of the Indies Museum. She was clutching a large box, a typewriter-paper box. Wilson assumed that this held the fruit of her long studies. When she disappeared into the cabin, Nacho turned.

"I was going to leave without you," he growled in English. "Where's the little girl and her mother?"

"Not coming," said the German.

Nacho turned to Wilson. "You said only two people."

"We are three," said the German, handing Nacho several bills. "And we want to have a nice trip, a fast trip."

The captain's eyes widened as he looked at the money. He pocketed it quickly.

"We will be in Cadiz by six in the morning, yes?" said the German.

The captain nodded. *"Si, señor!"* The money had made a distinct change in his manner. He motioned them onto the boat with a little bow.

Six in the morning. Maybe there was an Argentine or Brazilian freighter leaving then. Or, more likely, a German U-boat would be lying off Cadiz, waiting to take this great Teutonic leader to South America to join other Nazi criminals who had escaped the inevitable trials and noose.

The German smiled and jerked his head toward the boat. "After you, my dear Vice Consul."

Wilson looked back at the Cafe La Querencia. The German's hand was in the pocket of his raincoat. Still smiling, he added under his breath: "Any untoward movement, remember, and I kill you first, then the woman."

Wilson scanned the dock.

"Quickly!" the gunman said.

"Let her go home," said Wilson. "You've got me."

The German pushed the barrel of the pistol in his left pocket against her.

"Now!" he commanded. "On board!"

She stepped onto the gangplank and walked down it, followed by Wilson. The three crossed the covered deck, down the few steps into the main cabin.

A stench of fish, diesel fumes, and what smelled like rotten fruit assailed Wilson's nostrils when he entered.

It took a moment for his eyes to adjust; the only illumination came through the four small portholes. Then he made out other people there, seated on benches that ran around the sides of the cabin.

Miss Gold perched birdlike on the edge of a bench, holding her box to her chest. Next to her sat the black man, Moses Byrd, homburg hat tilted rakishly, both hands resting on the silver knob of his cane. Wilson's heart jumped when he saw him – an ally! Moses started to speak, but Wilson quickly shook his head, and Moses seemed to get the message. Had the German seen their look of recognition?

Across the cabin was a husky man of about forty, wearing a soiled seersucker jacket and a beret. Wilson recognized Sidney Phillips, American *matador,* one-time confidante and traveling companion of Ernest Hemingway. Wilson had often seen him in Los Corales Cafe on Sierpes Street, holding forth on his prowess in the arena in "those good old days" and predicting great things for his return to the taurine wars. In a happier situation, Wilson would have enjoyed talking about bullfighting with him.

Next to him sat a Spanish youth of fifteen or sixteen, well-dressed, aristocratic-looking. His moist red lips wore a pouty expression, and his thick black eyebrows almost grew together over heavy-lidded eyes. He looked as though he hadn't had a good night's sleep since kinder-garten.

The German took a seat in the corner of the cabin, up against the bulkhead, where he could survey the room and the entrance to it. The only other door was open, and Wilson could see it led to a small galley, a head, and the wheelhouse above.

The German motioned Gilly to sit next to him on his right, and Wilson next to her; he obviously wanted his left side, the pistol side, to have freedom of motion.

As Wilson sat down, Miss Gold nodded to him; they'd met at the Consulate's Fourth of July party, to which the few Americans in Sevilla were always invited. He remembered he'd enjoyed talking to the erudite, eccentric old woman.

The captain appeared.

"*Señores y señoras,* we go now," he said, adding in Spanish: "For those who should need the water closet, it is through the galley." He left the cabin for the bridge.

"What did he say?" the German asked.

Wilson translated, and as he did, he looked out of the porthole. No Moriarity!

The young girl Wilson had seen here on the boat in the morning appeared from the galley, carrying a tray with a bottle and seven glasses on it.

"Sherry, *señores,*" she said shyly. She had on too much makeup, but she was pretty.

"Refreshments, even!" said Phillips. "This sure is a first-class vessel!"

He didn't exactly say "foist," but there was Brooklyn in his accent.

When the girl stood in front of the young man, she cocked one hip and said coquettishly: "*Señorito,* do you care for our good sherry?"

The boy glanced at Phillips, who nodded. He took a glass without looking at the girl.

Phillips winked at the girl as he accepted the sherry. *"Eres ma' guapa que la mar!"* There was no Brooklyn in his Spanish, it was pure Andaluz. He turned toward Wilson and leaned forward to extend his hand.

"Hi," he said. "Sid Phillips, *Matador de Toros*. You look like a fellow American. And this is my nephew, Rafi."

Wilson shook his hand and said, "Wilson Tripp."

"Oh yeah!" said Phillips. "Heard about you, you're the guy who–" He looked unabashedly down at Wilson's leg.

"Couple of years ago," said Wilson. "Mexico."

"Gotta admire your guts, fella."

"Insanity," said Wilson, "more like it."

"Yeah, being an *espontáneo* with no training *is* sorta looney."

"Miss Gold here," the old woman said, holding out her fingers. "Formerly of Fall River, Mass., Lizzie Borden territory, forty whacks and so forth, and now from Sevilla. For four decades. I do have a first name, but along with everyone else I've forgotten it."

"And you are?" Phillips said, extending his hand.

The German didn't shake hands with Phillips. "Boyd," he said confidently. "Seymour Boyd."

"Hey," said Phillips. "Another American!"

"You're going to New York, Mr. Boyd?" said Miss Gold. "On *The Atlantic King*?"

The German barely hesitated. "Precisely," he said. "*The Atlantic King*."

"I'm sure you know," she said, "they've postponed the sailing till noon."

"Ah, yes," he said. "Of course, they so informed me."

Sure, they did, Wilson thought.

"We've plenty of time," she said.

"Quite so," he echoed. "Plenty of time."

Qvite zoh.

The black man said: "Moses Byrd at your service, Mr. Phillips. I saw you perform years ago."

"How was I?" Phillips brightened noticeably. "Pretty good?"

"Was in Barcelona," said Moses.

"Ears and tail, didn't I?"

"Guess it was an off day," said Moses.

"You got me confused, man!" Phillips frowned. "I always got at least one ear."

"Yessir," said Moses. "I just might be confused. Long time ago."

"Hell, El Gallo, the great Divine Baldy, used to follow me around, trying to learn how to do all this new stuff I brought to the spectacle." He looked at the boy. "Right, Rafi?"

The boy looked at him dully.

Phillips dug an elbow into the boy's side.

"Right, Rafi?"

The boy nodded. "Hokay," he said. "Hokay."

Wilson had the impression that that was the extent of the boy's English. Wilson looked out a porthole and saw that they were casting off the lines. He kept pleading for Moriarity to drive up. Where in God's name was he? All Moriarity would have to do would be to see him in the boat, size up the situation, and alert the British naval officers in Gibraltar, who would be delighted to apprehend the boat when it got to Cadiz or before.

"Do you realize that Columbus parked his ship right here, where we are now? On his return from his second voyage? Well, he did!" Miss Gold raised her glass of sherry. "Here's to the glorious end of a terrible war and the death finally of that awful man, Adolf Hitler."

Everyone drank except the German. He set his glass down and went to the entrance of the cabin, where the captain was removing the line from a cleat.

"We leave," said Nacho.

"No," said the German. "Wait."

Nacho started to protest – then dropped the rope and said nothing. The German came back and sat down.

Wilson didn't know what the delay was for, but so much the better, all the more time for Moriarity to arrive.

Miss Gold began jabbering.

"You're Jewish, aren't you, Mr. Phillips," she said. It was a statement more than a question.

"*Madame*," he said, "when you go into a bullfight, it's best to be of all religions."

"If you're Jewish," she persisted, "why do you wear that cross around your neck?"

"*Madame*," said Phillips with a toothy smile, "we are in Spain, and the bulls are Catholic."

"Idiotic remark," said Miss Gold. "You talk like that idiot Hemingway."

"*Madame*, where do you think he learned to talk that way?"

"Don't tell me about Hemingway, I knew him too. You know the old lady in *Death in the Afternoon*? That's me!" She snorted and turned from him to the German. She studied him. "Are you Jewish, sir?"

The German blinked but barely hesitated: "No, *madame*, I am not."

"Well, you look Jewish," Miss Gold said.

"I am American," said the man stiffly.

Good, keep going, thought Wilson, *hang yourself.*

"Well, hell's bells, mister, I'm American!" said Miss Gold. "But I'm also Jewish." She studied his face intently. "You know, you look familiar."

The German looked her back in the eyes. "I do, *madame?*"

"Yes, you do. You a senator or something famous?"

"No, *madame*, just a simple businessman."

"You have an accent."

"I went to school in Switzerland. When I was a child."

"Close to Germany," said Miss Gold, not completely satisfied. "But where are you from *now?*"

"From where?" echoed the German. "Now?"

"Where do you live in America?"

Yes, yes! Wilson thought. *Now the jig is up.*

"I am from," he hesitated, "Wilton–"

Yes, go on – Connect-it-cut will do it!

"Wilton?" interrupted Miss Gold. "Connecticut?"

The German nodded, relieved.

"Why," exclaimed Miss Gold, "my grandmother lived there when she was a girl!" Then she turned away from the German and said to Wilson, "You know, I'm very good at accents. You are from California. Probably Northern California."

"San Francisco," said Wilson. "Amazing."

"And you, Mr. Phillips, are from Brooklyn."

Phillips smiled. "That one's easy."

"Did you know Columbus was Jewish?" she asked.

"*Christopher* Columbus?" said Wilson.

"Yes, indeedy!" She patted the box which she clutched on her lap. "It's all in here. Took me years to dig up the proof, but I've finally got it all. The first clue was there was no priest on board. In those days, no ship would dream of setting out on a long voyage without a priest. But Columbus did! Three ships, some ninety men, no chaplain! Unheard of! The second clue is that the barber on board Columbus's ship was – guess what – also a rabbi!" She got up. "I take it the head is this way. Gotta spend a penny as we say in" – she looked at Gilly – "in your country, honey. London? Outside of London?"

Gilly smiled. "Right on, Miss Gold, Cricklewood to be exact."

As Miss Gold left the cabin, there was a squeal of brakes on the dock, the sound of tires skidding.

Moriarity! Wilson thought. He stood up.

Two figures appeared on the deck, but neither was the American clerk. They came down into the cabin. One was a large man, a huge man, the other much smaller, dressed in a gray trench coat with the collar up, dark glasses, and a beret. The small man clutched a briefcase as though life and immortal soul were locked inside. Wilson recognized the big man as his diplomatic counterpart, Klaus Stryker, the German Vice Consul; Wilson had met him only once, at a consular function, and only long enough for the German to insult Wilson personally and America in general. Stryker and the German glanced at each other and looked away quickly, with no sign of recognition, but Wilson heard the Vice Consul hiss something in German that sounded like *"sayshsteel."*

The Spanish girl went over to the little man. *"Señor,* do let me take your case and stow it for you."

The little man reacted like a patient in a dental chair when the drill hits a nerve.

"No, no," he exclaimed, turning and shielding the case as though it were a child in danger. Wilson saw that the handle was handcuffed to the man's wrist.

The German looked at the captain. "Now," he commanded, and Nacho nodded. Almost immediately, Wilson felt the boat throb, shudder, and glide away from the dock.

They were on their way. To where? To Cadiz – but then where? South America?

Miss Gold came back into the cabin and glared around as she sat down.

"Men," she told the world, "are very unspecific when they urinate – as long as they hit *something* they're happy."

Wilson studied the newcomers sitting on the far bench. Klaus, the Vice Consul, was a big florid man with a crew cut, huge shoulders, a thick neck, and forearms like Popeye. In America, he would have been a guard or maybe a fullback. The smaller man had hunched himself in the shadows of the corner, the briefcase against his chest, much the way Miss Gold hugged her manuscript box. It was hard to see his face with the beret down low, the dark glasses, and the coat collar up. But there was something familiar about him, something familiar about the shape of his head. The old Italian art professor at Yale who always spoke in exclamation points had once told him in portrait class: "Treep, you ask what ees most important, the mouth or the eyes for the likeness! And I must tell you, neither! Most important first ees shape of head! Eef you see a picture of jus' an eye or jus' the leeps of your sweetsheart, you not recognize her! But eef you see silhouette! Ah hah! You recognize her at once by shape of head!"

And so it was now. The shape of this man's head, the length of the half-hidden face. Who was he? Someone important, because Klaus was obviously here to escort and protect him, not the German. Someone important, because there was a bulge under Klaus's breast pocket. A diplomat carrying a pistol? Someone very important. What man would be more important than Martin Bormann – if that's who this German was – that the German Consulate would have orders to protect and escort to a safe haven, such as Argentina via Sevilla and Cadiz?

Hess was in jail, Himmler and Hitler suicides. Goering, von Ribbentrop, and the rest of Hitler's gang had been apprehended and were awaiting trial. There was no German more important than Bormann – if indeed this was Bormann.

Unless this little man was the world-famous scientist Hans Roediger.

Wilson felt the back of his neck tingle.

Could this insignificant figure possibly be the dread Roediger, Albert Einstein's teacher, the most feared scientist in the world? The man Werner von Braun had learned rocketry from? Who had invented the Roediger bombsight and who, rumors said, had come up with an invention to nullify all radar? Only the sudden end of the war had prevented its being put into practice. Other rumors said that he, along with Werner Heisenberg, had developed the most devastating bomb the world had ever known.

Wasn't it possible, just as the German had made his way through France and Spain, that this man could have also – prudently, separately, and via a different route – arrived here? Why Cadiz? Because it was on the Atlantic and the German sub would be lying there, waiting for them tomorrow, all prearranged. Roediger's destination would probably be Tokyo, not Argentina. The war with Japan was still very much on, the final outcome still in doubt.

No wonder the German had said this trip was more important than anyone could know. Perhaps the answers were in that briefcase handcuffed to the wrist of the little man across from him.

The boat was already in the middle of the river now and making good time. Miss Gold had replenished her sherry. "Well, off we go," she said, raising her glass. "Off to Canterbury!"

Wilson took a sip of sherry.

"Colombo, means dove," said Miss Gold. "When he went to Portugal, he was called Colom. In Spain, he called himself first Coloma, then Colón. His real name was Cristoforo Colombo."

"Man, Miss Gold, you must be the world's greatest expert on that guy," Moses Byrd said.

"Bullshit," said Miss Gold. "I don't know diddly-squat about Columbus."

"But you've been studying him in the Archivos de las Indias for so many years," said Wilson.

"Bullshit, I've been tracking down the lives of *la tripulación,* and that's all."

"His crew?"

She nodded and patted the manuscript box. "All eighty-six of them. I've recorded almost all of their names and lives, all right in here, ready for the publisher."

"No Columbus stuff?" Moses asked.

"Poor old Chris," she said, shaking her head. "He didn't have the slightest idea where he was going when he left, he didn't know where he was when he got there, and he didn't know where the hell he'd been when he returned."

"And you are further saying," said Moses, "that this great ship captain was a Jewish gentleman?"

"So what's the big deal?" Miss Gold snorted. "Wasn't Noah?"

Jesus, where was Moriarity? If he didn't show up, didn't see the boat, didn't call O.S.S., didn't alert Gibraltar, didn't get the picture – they were cooked.

9

After hearing his wife's cry for help, Moriarity raced back through the Consulate office, then out and across the patio, into the door leading to the residences. He took the stairs two at a time, arriving at the door of his apartment just as it opened. Domingo, the Consulate handyman, lurched out, carrying his wooden trough of tools. A short, middle-aged man with a kind face and a large mustache, Domingo wore overalls. His shirt was torn, and there were scratch marks down one side of his face. He looked stricken as Moriarity grabbed him by the collar.

"I swear, *señor*," he gasped, "I did nothing!"

"What happened?" Moriarity asked, but he already knew. It would be like the time three months ago with the State Department courier, and five months before that with the gardener, and before that…

"I swear by the Macarena, I only came up to fix the sink," Domingo gasped for breath, "when suddenly the *señora* – like a mad woman–"

"I know," Moriarity spoke quietly, releasing the man.

"I did not ask the *señora* to take off her clothes, I swear! When I opened the door she–"

"Shut up, man," said Moriarity. He took a hundred-peseta note from his pocket and shoved it down the front of Domingo's overalls. "Don't discuss this with anyone, understand?"

"*Si, señor,*" mumbled Domingo, fishing out the bill. "I am a happily married man, *señor,* I want you to know that!"

Moriarity pushed past him and strode into the apartment.

Colette, still with no clothes on, flung herself into his arms, sobbing.

"Poochie, he tried to fawk me!"

He held her close and stroked her hair gently, as he would a child's. "There, there, Cherie," he said. "It's all right, everything's all right. Domingo's a good man."

"I swear he ripped my clothes off!" she sobbed. "He was going to do it to me! Just like in Berlin!" She smelled strongly of lilac perfume.

"Buck up, m'girl," Moriarity whispered. "It's all right."

Her body tensed with fear. "You won't send me back to that place again, will you, Poochie?"

"No, darling."

"You promise?"

He nodded, and he meant it. Never again to that snake pit, where they gave her shock treatments that did no good, and sprayed her with a fire hose, and gave her endless sessions with doctors who couldn't understand her problem in a million years.

"Say it!"

"I promise, darling."

She managed a smile. He picked her up, twirled her twice around the room, and laid her gently on the bed.

"It was so terrible, Poochie," she said, but in a different voice now, a coy little-girl voice. She took his hand and put it on one breast.

"That man. He touched me here," she moved his hand to her other breast, "and here," she moved his hand down, "and even here. Come to bed, Poochie."

"Later, darling," he said.

"I want you in me," she said.

He flung himself off the bed.

"I must go."

"But Poochie—"

Backing away, he blew her a kiss at the door and was gone.

Moriarity hurried out to his Ford sedan and jumped in. Though ten years old, the vehicle was one of the better privately owned cars in war-deprived Sevilla.

He was able to drive fast along the river because there was little traffic on Paseo de las Delicias at this hour. Then he raced across the San Telmo bridge to Triana, took a sharp left turn which took him along the quay, and finally he skidded to a stop in front of the little bar and gas station. The sign over the door was missing the wooden cut-out letter "R" in Querencia.

Moriarity looked at his watch as he got out of the car. It was well after the appointed time, but there was no one at the outdoor tables. He went inside.

The bartender-owner, Facundo Montero, was at the end of the bar. Behind him on the wall hung a life-size oil painting of himself in the Sevilla bullring after one of his triumphal afternoons, one of his very few triumphal afternoons. It was hard to find the young golden boy of the picture in the fat, hair-combed-over-bald-pate, old man cutting a salami for *tapas* for the evening clientele that would soon be drifting in; Moriarity noticed that he was using an up-and-down chop, like finishing off a bull with a *puntilla*, rather than a conventional slice.

"*Hola,*" grunted the old man.

"*Hola.*" Moriarity looked around the room, whose walls were crowded with bulls' heads, gaudy fading posters, and photos of Facundo; everywhere were fly-specked photos of Facundo – alone in action or standing with Joaquín Del Monte or Joselito or Sánchez Mejías. But Wilson was not in the bar.

"*Matador,*" said Moriarity, "have you seen the Vice Consul?"

"The usual?" said Facundo, starting to pour a shot glass of Fundador. "My father always told me that if it weren't for alcohol, a poor man would never know how a rich man feels, and that was good enough for me."

"The Vice Counsul!"

Moriarity shook his head, but the man had already filled the glass and one for himself. "This is important, man. Has he been here?"

"Not today. You don't want this?"

Moriarity hesitated.

"You sick?" said Facundo, drinking.

Moriarity took the shot glass and threw back the drink. "I was born–" started Moriarity.

"Two drinks under par," Facundo finished.

There was a squeal of brakes, and a car skidded to a stop. As he went outside, Moriarity saw the big German Vice Consul hurry by. He was headed for the boats. Trotting by his side was a little man with a beret and dark glasses. He was clutching a briefcase, and the late afternoon sun glinted off the handcuffs that attached it to his right wrist.

Did these two have something to do with Wilson's problem?

Moriarity followed them at a discreet distance. The two men were too intent on their destination to notice him. The men passed two boats and stopped in front of the *Cayetana*. Immediately after they boarded, the gangplank was hauled over onto the deck of the seedy craft and the captain and a girl cast off the ropes.

Moriarity ran down to the edge of the dock as the boat, its motor grumbling, glided away. Through one of the portholes he could see Miss Gold, the old historian whose passport he'd renewed recently, and next to her the darkness of old Moses Byrd. Another porthole framed what looked like the back of Wilson's head. Moriarity was almost sure it was Wilson. What the hell was he doing on this boat? The boat was too far out for him to jump aboard, and calling to Wilson could accomplish nothing.

Then Moriarity saw *him*. Next to Wilson was another head, a Teutonic head.

The *Cayetana* was now ten feet from the dock and starting to pick up speed. He could barely make out what he knew were deep-set, pale blue eyes. Moriarity felt a clutch in his stomach as he stared at the man. He had seen eyes just like those blue murderous eyes before, and he knew exactly where. They were the eyes of every Nazi he'd seen in Berlin and Munich; they were the eyes of the men who had raped his wife.

He ran back toward his car. Between Sevilla and Cadiz there was one bridge over the Guadalquivir River. He had to get to that bridge before the boat did. But a weapon? What would he do for a weapon?

10

When Mia von Wurmbrandt de Alvarez left her dead daughter in the apartment, fury had supplanted grief. As she rushed down the street in a blind rage, she thought: *Get to the boat before it pulled away from the dock, take the little pistol from the pocket of the dress, and shoot the murderer dead.* Only then could she accept the girl's death and try to understand it.

She dreaded the call she'd have to make to her mother-in-law, who adored Heidi and who had been sure that the new miracle drug would cure the little girl. The old woman was still trying to deal with the fact that her son, Luis, had been missing from the Blue Division for six months and perhaps lay dead at the Russian front, along with thousands of other idealistic Spaniards and Germans.

Now Mia was running down the sidewalk, brushing past people, pushing them out of the way, the scarf tight about her wounded head, her hand clutching the pistol in the pocket of the shabby black dress she'd taken from the maid's closet. Dressed this way she might be able to get closer to him before she shot him. She would shove the pistol up against his chest! She would pull the trigger! She would not miss!

But then she slowed down.

Was this really the way to accomplish what she wanted? Perhaps legal capture, humiliation before the world, and formal execution would be worse punishment; there was already talk of a tribunal and criminal proceedings for war crimes. Besides, she knew little of guns and nothing of violence; suppose she bungled the job and injured someone else, perhaps even Wilson, of whom she was becoming so fond.

She turned and hurried down General Franco Street to a two-story building. Outside, under a flagpole and the seal of Germany, was a sign: *Consulado de Alemania.*

At the door, two men, obviously in a hurry, shoved her aside on their way out. One was a small man whom she didn't know, a briefcase handcuffed to his wrist. The other was a huge man she knew and despised: Klaus Stryker, the German Vice Consul. From a Nazi family and a dedicated Nazi himself, he'd been in the army briefly, until wounded. Some said he'd shot himself in the foot to get away from the Russian front. He had been rejected even by the Gestapo, and had ended up here in the Consulate. He was from Halberstadt, the murderer's, the German's, hometown, so surely he'd been aided by him in getting himself into the Consular Corps. Klaus had come to Mia's apartment on some pretext when he first arrived in Sevilla ("We Germans must stick together"), and she'd tried to be nice to him. She gave him a nice dinner, and afterward he'd tried to rape her. Only the arrival of Mia's mother-in-law and daughter had saved her. She'd not seen him since.

She pulled the shawl across her face as Klaus's bulk brushed past. But he was in too much of a hurry to notice, and she quickly ducked into the Consulate.

The big office was smoky and in chaos. Three clerks were bustling about. One was yanking open file cabinets and carrying papers to the center of the room, where a brass charcoal brazier awaited them.

Standing straight and supervising this was Consul General Dieter Schmidt. Tall and aristocratic, with a large gray mustache, he was dressed like a tweedy English country squire; indeed, he'd graduated from Harrow before going to Heidelberg and entering the Consular Corps. On his head, incongruously, perched a Tyrolean hat. Under his watery blue eyes were great circles, and he wore a haggard, half-beaten, half-frightened look. Mia had met him here in Sevilla at various social functions, knew relatives of his in Germany, and found him to be a cultivated and charming "gentleman of the old school,

B.H." Before Hitler.

She started to approach him, but a fat clerk puffed up between them, carrying a large drawer. In it were dozens of red felt armbands with black swastikas.

"And what of these, Herr Konsul? We save?"

The Consul merely pointed at the small fire. Then he saw Mia.

She started toward the Consul, but a white-haired woman approached, holding up an oil portrait of Hitler in military uniform.

"And this, Herr Konsul?"

The Consul frowned and jabbed a finger twice at the fire. "*There,*" he growled, "is the place for the root of all our troubles."

"Please," said the woman. "May I keep it?"

The Consul shook his head in wonderment. "Anna, whatever for?"

"Herr Konsul, he was a good man, he was our leader."

The Consul snorted, sighed, and rubbed his mustache. "Take it then, Anna, take it, but what on earth–"

"Herr Schmidt!" broke in Mia. "I must speak with you immediately!"

He looked at her with rheumy eyes. "Aren't you–"

"Mia von Wurmbrandt. My husband is Luis Alvarez. I must talk to you."

The intensity in her voice demanded his attention. He took in her shawl and shabby dress, said nothing, but gestured to an office. She followed him into a spacious room with a large desk piled high with files. On one wall was a large photo, askew, of a benign Hitler, the official portrait that hung in every German Consulate in every major city of the neutral world. On the wall behind his desk was a pastoral painting of a Bavarian trout stream, and on another was a print of Durer's praying hands. Over the door was a mounted stag's head, and below that an ornately engraved shotgun rested across two deer's feet.

"My dear," he said, sitting down behind his desk and putting an unlit pipe in his mouth, "You look terribly distraught."

"He is here!" she almost shouted.

The Consul took the pipe out of his mouth and leaned forward. "Who?"

"You know who – my godfather!" She didn't want to say his name. "The murderer!"

His jaw dropped and his eyes widened.

"I heard rumors, but–"

"He murdered my daughter!" Her voice broke and she pointed to her head. "And he tried to kill me."

"My God! When?"

"Less than an hour ago."

She put her face in her hands and her shoulders shook. But she must not break down now, she must not give in to the grief. Time for that later.

"Be stoic, my dear," he said. "We must all be stoic in these times." He rose, came to where she sat, and put an arm around her. "My poor Mia. Sit."

"No, no!" she said fiercely, dragging the back of her hand across her tears. "We must do something. *You* must do something! He's escaping! Probably to South America. Maybe to Japan – to help the Japanese prolong this horrible war – who knows. You must do something quickly!"

He returned to his swivel chair and blew out a sigh. "What would you have me do, dear Mia?"

"He's on a boat going to Cadiz! Stop him!"

The Consul sighed deeply again. "I am alone here now. Klaus has gone off in a hurry – gone somewhere without telling me. I don't know what he's up to. Berlin has put him up to something very mysterious."

"Arm yourself and we will go after him!"

"Diplomats do not have weapons, you know that."

She pointed at the shotgun under the stag's head. His eyes narrowed and he growled: "Don't be foolish, woman! It's for grouse!" He sounded more frustrated than angry. "You wish me to go after a notoriously dangerous Nazi with an ancient fowling piece?"

"Then warn the German Consulate in Cadiz!"

"There is none there."

She pounded the desk. "What can we do?"

"Have you gone to the Spanish police?"

"They will say 'we are a neutral country, we do not interfere.'"

"But if a murder has been committed–"

"By the time they fill out the forms, talk it over with General Franco, and have a glass of sherry, the man will be aboard a submarine in the Atlantic! Please, oh God, please!"

"Have you tried the American or British Consulates?"

he asked. "It is they who want to hang him, not me. I am not a Nazi and never have been, but it is not my place to capture Nazis."

She rose to go. "I hoped I would find more help from a fellow German."

"I am truly sorry, my dear. Try the American Consul. His wife's German, Ingrid Farben she was, from Frankfurt."

"My dear godfather said my brother, Max, has been killed. Did you know anything about this?"

The Consul shook his head mournfully. "So many being killed in Germany these days. Your brother? I am sorry. Your Uncle Wilhelm, of course, was killed after the attempt on Hitler's life."

She'd never been close to her uncle, especially after he became part of Hitler's coterie of generals. But his death, hanged alive on a meat hook along with his fellow conspirators, the whole action filmed for a gleeful Hitler to play and replay, was too horrible to contemplate.

"Before I go," Mia hesitated, "May I ask you one last thing, Herr Schmidt?"

"Surely, Mia dear."

"I happen to know the American Vice Consul, and the other day he told me the Allies had liberated camps, dozens of camps, 'concentration camps' he called them. Even showed me films. Were they faked?"

The Consul shifted in his chair. "We called them 'relocation camps,'" he said uncomfortably.

"So it is true, then."

"What is true?"

"That they existed. I told him I didn't believe him."

"They existed."

"But they – they didn't kill people there? Jews and Gypsies and Poles? In ovens and by gas? Did they?"

The Consul closed his eyes.

"By the hundreds?" she said.

He didn't say anything.

"By the – thousands?" she said weakly.

He opened his eyes. "By the millions," he said flatly. "They gave it a charming name – *Endlösung* – the Final Solution."

"Oh, God," she whispered. She clenched her fists. "And I called him a liar! I said he was a victim of his country's propaganda."

She was silent for a moment. "Herr Schmidt, are we Germans some species of monsters?"

"No, my dear," he said gently. "We are a great, artistic, and noble race. It is the Nazis – an aberration."

She slammed her palm on the desk.

"And one of the worst of those Nazis is getting away free right now!" she said.

The Consul was staring off into space now.

"If you could only have seen the Germany I knew – the wonderful Germany before the First World War. It was paradise. You know, my dear, I, too, was shocked when I heard about the camps, found it hard to believe, monstrous even. But you know something?"

He swiveled his chair around and looked up at her

with his watery eyes. "I do not condone those camps, of course, nor the suffering that went on, nor the Nazi methods. But really, Mia, when you think about it," he smiled a sad smile, "all things being equal–" he brushed a forefinger across his mustache. "Isn't Germany and the world a better place without *those* people?"

Mia backed away from his desk. At the door she pointed her trembling finger at him. "Damn you," she said between clenched teeth. "Damn you to hell!"

She turned and fled from the building, hailing the first taxi she saw.

11

The *Cayetana* was in the middle of the river now and making good knots. Sevilla was far behind them, the tip of the Giralda Tower barely visible on the horizon. They'd passed the cluster of white houses that was Gines, and now they were leaving the village of Gelves behind.

"Birthplace of Joselito!" the *matador* Sid Phillips pointed and announced to the group of passengers. "You know who he was, don't you, Mister Vice Consul?"

Across the cabin, Wilson said, "According to Hemingway, the greatest *matador* who ever lived, right?"

"Wrong," said Phillips. "Second-greatest." He turned to Moses Byrd. "George, who's the greatest?"

Moses hesitated, then deadpanned, "Manolete? Del Monte?"

Phillips made a mock swipe at the man's gray head. "Me, buster, me! If for no other reason than Joselito got himself killed by a bull when he was twenty-five. I'm still alive."

"You almost got yourself killed, though," Wilson said. "I read that in *Death in the Afternoon*."

Phillips needed no more prompting. With a glance at the young, pouty boy by his side, he pulled up his shirt, revealing a great scar like a big zipper running across his abdomen. "Can't show you the really bad one."

Miss Gold and Miss Leigh-Jones gasped. The thick-lipped boy yawned.

"Just part of the profession, ladies," said Phillips. "Every *matador* gets gored to some degree, about once a season. Some are luckier than others, that's all."

The young girl was passing sherry again, and it was like a jolly outing on the river. Except that Wilson was sitting on a bench with a Nazi murderer. The man who'd shot Mia and her daughter. The man who probably would kill him when he was no longer aiding his escape. Who *certainly* would kill him.

Wilson had never seriously contemplated his own death before, how it would be, even when he'd been gored in the leg in Mexico City. Now he remembered, from his university class, "Psych 66," the disturbing paragraph of Freud's. No one can truly imagine his or her own death; one always envisions oneself there as an observer and around for the subsequent scenes.

He'd been given that paragraph on a test, been

instructed to critique it; he'd done badly, not knowing what to write. He'd do better now, much better. Wilson thought of his mother weeping quietly at his funeral, his old grandfather, the judge, his arm around her, his sister coming in from—

"Lovely evening," said a voice, an ironical voice of forced airiness.

It was the English girl, Gilly. She'd barely uttered more than two sentences since they'd been taken hostage.

"Yes," said Wilson, trying to match her tone, "Isn't it just."

The girl gave a sidelong glance at the German.

"I never get used to the sun's being around so late in Spain. Do you, Mister Tripp?"

He looked at his watch. It was after eight o'clock. "No," he said.

"Any," she said casually, in measured tones, "ideas?"

The German's head turned toward them, alert to their every word.

"No," said Wilson. "No ideas."

They were helpless. If Wilson had had any Boy Scout schemes of overpowering or neutralizing their captor, he'd abandoned them when Klaus Stryker came aboard. The bulge in Stryker's right coat pocket appeared to be a pistol. So it was two armed men, at least one of them desperate, against – what? Wilson and who else?

He looked across the deck at Moses Byrd, whose hands and chin rested on his silver-headed cane as he listened, smiling drowsily, to whatever Miss Gold was talking about. Columbus, for sure.

Moses would certainly be on Wilson's side, but he was old. Sidney Phillips was his big hope. He was fit, and of course, as a *matador,* he'd be brave. His fat young boy friend was useless. The captain would be of no help, he was half-drunk already and perhaps was pro-German. The German's money, alone, made him pro-German.

What were the other options?

The only one Wilson could think of was to jump overboard, try to stay under long enough to avoid the bullets, then make the long swim to shore and go for help. But help where?

Not a very good idea.

I was not born to be a Hemingway hero, Wilson thought. *I should have learned that when I got clobbered by that bull in Mexico.*

"I once saw a cartoon," Gilly was saying, "probably in *Punch* or your *New Yorker.* It showed two men in a dungeon, manacled hand and foot, spread-eagled up on a wall, and one says to the other: 'Now here's my plan!'" She gave a mirthless laugh. "That's the way I see us now."

The German turned and said under his breath:

"You will be quiet!"

"Or what?" Gilly shot back in a low voice.

"Quiet!" commanded the German, maintaining a smile for anyone looking, as he put his left hand in his pocket significantly.

"Are you going to shoot me?" Gilly said. "Go ahead, shoot me."

The German glared at her but said nothing.

"Look at those beauties," said Sidney Phillips. "Man, this is true bull country!"

On the right side of the river, they were passing fields filled with huge bulls. These were bigger and more beautiful than the ones Wilson had encountered in Mexico. They were clearly fighting bulls, resembling their domestic cousins only in the way a wolf resembles a German shepherd. These were wild animals in every sense of the word.

"This is the famous Concha y Sierra Ranch," said Phillips. "Very dangerous animals. They've killed almost as many bullfighters as the Miuras, including the great Pascual Márquez."

Most of these bulls were black, some were dark brown, a few were pinto, but all were *toros bravos,* that special breed of animal originally found only on the Iberian peninsula and bred for centuries for one purpose: to try to kill men.

Phillips was saying: "Folks, you're looking at the most perfect living instruments for killing that man has been able to devise."

He went on, a familiar and beloved theme to him, the core of his being, these wild, anachronistic animals.

"Weigh at least half a ton, turn faster than a polo pony, and can beat any race horse alive for the first hundred yards."

For years, these animals had led perfect lives after having been picked for the arena, Phillips told them; their unfortunate brethren had gone to the slaughterhouse at a year-and-a-half. For four years, these massive specimens of sculpted muscle had done nothing but eat and fight among themselves and grow strong, awaiting the twenty-minute justification for their existence, in an arena in Spain or Portugal or even in southern France. They were *bred* to fight; no one needed to train them to charge any more than one needed to train a rattlesnake to strike. Never molested or tortured, they would not encounter a man who was not on horseback until their day in the arena. The only dismounted people they would see were those passing on the riverboats, like the *Cayetana*.

"See that *cornigacho* on the right there?" said Sidney, pointing at a bull with down-curving horns. "That's like the one I fought in Madrid in twenty-nine, the one they gave me the ear for."

"I swear," Moses said, "I don't understand how you have the guts to face one of those guys."

"Will Rogers said something like 'we're all ignorant but on different subjects,'" said Phillips. "And I say we're all cowards, but about different things. For instance, I wouldn't have the courage to go to an office every day of my life. And I'm afraid of snakes. Bulls I like."

"I know you've both been wounded in the arena," said Gilly, looking at Sidney and then at Wilson, "and I'm sorry, but I'm afraid I always root for the bull."

"That shows you like animals better than humans," said Sidney, taking no offense.

"I came to *that* conclusion a long time ago," said Gilly.

"Bullfighting is indefensible," Wilson volunteered,

"but irresistible."

Wilson was surprised that she knew about his leg. He wondered how.

"Hey, pretty Miss," Sidney said to Gilly. "Do you know your hair, that white streak, it's just like Manolete's?"

Gilly smiled. "Everyone has told me that since I came to Spain. Quite a distinction, apparently."

"But you're a lot prettier than he is!" said Sidney.

"Nice to know that," she said.

Now they saw bulls in the fields on both sides of the river. Incredibly, big white egrets perched on the backs of some of the animals. A few bulls were at the river's edge, drinking up their reflections.

"And that black-and-white one over there," Sidney was telling the German Vice Consul, who clearly wasn't listening, "that's like the one I triumphed with in Barcelona."

Gilly stood up.

"You are going where?" demanded the German.

"With your so very kind permission," – she spat out the words – "I'm going to the loo."

"Loo?" said the German.

"W.C., *toilette*, can, necessarium," she said and strode out of the main cabin.

The German glared after her trim figure.

"Arrogant English bitch," he growled. Then he added ominously: "We will see, we will see."

The young girl appeared again, bearing a tray of *serrano* ham slices and the bottle of sherry. Miss Gold was the first to hold out her glass. The German took several slices of ham, had her fill his glass, tossed it down, and held it out again for a refill.

Atta boy, thought Wilson, *get yourself loaded, go to sleep, and I'll take your gun away from you. Let's see how brave you are without your Lüger, you fucking Nazi murderer.*

The German Vice Consul, Klaus Stryker, who had not spoken up till now, raised his glass of sherry.

"*Prosit,*" he said, unsmiling, in a high voice that did not seem to belong to the man's big body.

Miss Gold lifted her glass and said something in German.

"You speak German?" Wilson asked.

"I speak six languages," she said. "But so what – so does every head waiter."

The German raised his sherry. "Cheers," he said.

"*Prosit,*" said the boy.

He lifted his glass and drank. Of course, being the son of a *marqués,* he would be pro-German; most of Spain's aristocracy had been *Germanófilo* if only because they were so terrified of the very real threat of Communism. They felt a debt to Hitler for his military support of Franco during the Spanish Civil War. Phillips glared at him but said nothing.

Miss Gold drank and drank again. She was a little tipsy when she turned to the German and said: "Mr. Boyd?"

The German looked at her warily. "Yes?"

"Mr. Boyd, I've been working on your accent. Real challenge, that accent of yours. You say you went to school in Switzerland. Okay, but what I hear is pure Germany."

"Germany?" he exclaimed, as though she'd said Mars.

"Somewhere around Hamburg," she ruminated. "Maybe near, yes, near Halberstadt."

The German winced slightly. He and Klaus Stryker exchanged glances briefly. Then the German forced a smile.

"My grandparents came–"

"Bullshit," Miss Gold snapped. "People don't acquire an accent from their grandparents." She looked hard at the German. "You look very familiar to me for some reason."

"I can assure you, *madame*, we have not met."

Why in the world did people not know what Martin Bormann looked like immediately? Everyone knew what Hess, with the Groucho Marx eyebrows, looked like. And Goering, a depraved, bloated exploded haggis. And Goebbels, looking more emaciated and skeletal than his worst concentration victim.

But Bormann? Wilson saw in his mind's eye only a broad face and dark eyes in the published photos.

Miss Gold drank and stared sadly into space. "My parents were from Hamburg. I was born in America, like my sister and her husband. But they went back to live out their days in Hamburg. I was so worried when the Allies bombed the city flat." She gave a bitter laugh. "I needn't have worried. Oh, sure, they were safe from the bombing, but they'd been taken to Dachau and ended up in a Nazi oven."

The German shrugged uncomfortably. "*Madame,* I can't–"

"Doesn't matter!" Miss Gold went suddenly morose. She stared into her newly-filled glass and rambled. "Nothing matters a great deal. When you come right down to it, we shouldn't lend importance to the human plight or the mystery of the whither bound. When you think that a million marbles the size of our planet could fit into the sun and the sun is a mere pinpoint among millions of colossal stars, it's hard to feel that human affairs have the least importance beyond each of our own heres and nows." She hiccupped and a tear trickled down her cheek. "All our remains must end in a soon-forgotten grave as a – as a lifeless submicrocosm that in time dissolves and scatters and is forever lost, just as surely as the stoutest of tombstones." She clutched her manuscript to her bosom as though it were a suckling babe, drank more sherry, and said: "All I have in this wretched solar system to console me is the crew of this Jewish-Italian explorer."

Moses reached over and patted her hand. "Surely not so bad as all that, Miss Gold."

Miss Gold suddenly put her chin down on her chest and went to sleep.

"Hey, Boyd," said Phillips amiably from across the cabin, "What're you doing in Spain?" Then: "Boyd?"

There was only a slight delay as the German realized Phillips was speaking to him.

"Sherry," he replied. "Sherry business."

"Of course, you import from Jerez. Know my friend Alvaro Domecq?"

"Doesn't everyone?" said the German with a smile.

Good bluff, Wilson thought.

"Hell of a *rejoneador,* eh?"

The German nodded. "Quite so."

Hell, he doesn't even know what a rejoneador is, thought Wilson.

"You've seen him perform?" Phillips pursued.

"Who?" the German stalled.

"Domecq."

"Sometimes," he said evasively. "Quite so."

To avoid further questions, he was quick to stand up when Gilly reclaimed to her seat on the bench.

"You have returned," said the German, and gave her his charming smile.

"Qvite zoh," Gilly said curtly, imitating the German's accent expertly.

The German glared at her.

"Say, Boyd," said Phillips, "our friend Domecq is going to appear next month on the same program with me – my comeback fight. Course, he's fighting Portuguese-style, on horseback. Manolete will probably be on the same program."

Oh, sure, thought Wilson, *the great Spaniard appearing with this washed-up, over-the-hill American.*

"I might decide to fight some of these Concha y Sierra bulls over there," Phillips said. "If I can find some really big ones."

Come on, thought Wilson.

He felt a nudge.

"Jimmy, you might find it a nice *idea*, Jimmy," said Gilly, "if you *engineered* a trip to the loo."

Wilson looked at her blankly.

"What are you talking?" demanded the German.

"I simply remarked," she said, "that it was a nice idea to have made a trip to the loo. Does that offend Your Royal Rectum?"

The German's fierce eyes stared hard at her. He muttered something in German, then he turned his head away.

Gilly took off her dark glasses and looked meaningfully at Wilson. For the first time, Wilson saw that she had beautiful green eyes under her thick brows. She was frowning, signaling. He obviously was supposed to do something, understand something. But what? And why did she call him Jimmy? She gave a slight movement of her head toward where she'd come from – the head.

He got up. "Bathroom," he announced. The German nodded.

Wilson walked across the cabin to the open door that led forward. He went through the little galley where the young girl was making sandwiches. She smiled coquettishly at him. Then the passageway narrowed into the engine room. Half of the hatch was lifted up, and he could see the workings of the engine pumping away noisily. Ahead of him he made out the back of the captain at the wheel. At the left was a door with porcelain letters affixed on it: *SERVICIOS*. He looked down at the working of the engine before he went into the head.

It was a cramped closet with only a pump-type toilet and a small basin. He looked around the space, examining the walls, the ceiling, and the back of the toilet's wooden lid. No note, nothing.

What had she said besides "nice idea"?

Engineered. And the funny way she had said it, dividing it into two very distinct syllables: *Engine*-eered. And she had called him Jimmy twice. Was she nuts?

Then he understood. The plan. Jimmy the engine. Yes! Then the boat stops! We float helplessly until picked up by authorities, who take the German into custody. Clever girl.

But how to jimmy the engine and with what? If he were to simply rip out some wires, the German would know, would shoot him, the captain would repair the boat, and the German would continue merrily on his way to freedom.

Wilson didn't know much about motors, but he remembered staying with a friend at Lake Tahoe once in his teens. They'd set out to cross the lake in the family's classic Gar-Wood inboard, and the boat had run only a few minutes before conking out. It turned out that, in a fit of pique, his friend's kid brother had cut the small hose that ran from the fuel filter to the carburetor. It had taken a day to fix the engine.

But how to cut the hose? Then he thought of his knife.

He put the lid down, sat on the toilet, took down his

pants, and slid down his brace.

"Good old Betsy," he said as he extracted the knife.

He slipped the knife into his jacket pocket, pulled up the brace and his trousers, went out of the toilet, and closed the door behind him. He walked down the passageway to where the engine was chunking away. It was a Chrysler Marine, almost like the one in his friend's boat, but an older model. And yes, he could just see a six-inch yellow hose, about an inch thick, running from the fuel filter to the carburetor, upon which the engine's life depended. One swipe of the knife would do it, then back to his seat, looking innocent. Five minutes later, the fuel in the carburetor would be used up, the motor would sputter, and Mister Good German's Excellent River Excursion would be at an end.

The girl was still in the galley, unable to see him; the captain had his back to him. He could do it now.

He had the knife eased out of his pocket when he looked up suddenly and saw the German standing before him in the passageway.

"Come quickly!" he commanded. "Police, the police are coming."

Wilson followed him back to the main cabin.

"Sit!" whispered the German. Behind them Wilson saw, approaching fast, a black boat with *Guardia* written large on its side in white letters. Two *guardia* officers with automatic rifles slung from their shoulders stood on the bow in their green uniforms, their black patent-leather hats glistening in the glare off the water.

"We're saved!" Gilly breathed.

"These guys are tough," said Wilson. "The toughest."

The German's left hand went to his jacket pocket. He prodded the barrel of the pistol into Wilson's side. Then he took his hand out and put it firmly on Wilson's shoulder.

"Do not make with excitement, Mister American," he whispered. "Let's all live. Do not play the hero. You cannot win — we are Germans. Remember, if you say or do anything wrong, you die first, then she dies. At the same time, Klaus will take care of the police."

The police boat drew alongside, its rubber-tire fenders bumping hard against the *Cayetana*.

"We're saved," Gilly said again.

"Yes," said Wilson. "Maybe."

"And maybe not," the German said calmly under his breath. His eyes were fixed on the two Guardia Civil officers as they slipped the straps of their short automatic rifles off their shoulders and prepared to come aboard.

Wilson saw the German's hand straying toward his pocket. *What's this maniac going to do,* he thought, *kill them all? And then us?*

12

Mia hailed the first taxi she saw, one of the few in Sevilla; due to the war-caused shortage of gasoline, the only non-horse cabs operating these days were *"gasógenos,"* ancient taxies with a huge, ingenious apparatus that looked like a water heater mounted on the back. They ran on coal or wood, no one seemed to know just how. But they ran.

Before the old driver could ask for a destination, Mia cried out as she jumped into the rear seat: "American Consulate. Quickly!"

The car lurched off.

"As you wish, *señorita,* we will go to the American Consulate," said the driver, "but just how quickly depends entirely on *Rosinante* here."

They'd only gone a hundred yards before the car coughed twice and glided to a stop.

"*Qúe pasa?*" Mia groaned.

"*Rosinante* wants his dinner," said the driver mournfully. "*Rosinante* is hungry, hungry all the time. *Rosinante,* raised on gasoline, mother's milk, doesn't understand this new horrible diet. It, excuse me, *señorita,* but it constipates him."

The driver got out, grabbed some briquettes from a gunny sack roped on the roof of the car, walked to the rear of the vehicle, and fed them into the bottom of the tank. Back at the wheel, he started up the car, revved up the motor, and, with lurches, belches, and flatulence the car set off, eventually at a respectable pace, passing several carriages as they went through a corner of María Luisa Park.

Mia noticed many fancy carriages as well as official sedans, mostly Mercedes Benzes, Hispano Suizas, and Fiats, all heading for the Exhibition Hall of the park.

"The big official reception for Franco," the driver explained and spat out the window. "May he rot in hell."

"Driver, are you going as fast as you can?" Mia asked.

"*Señorita,* I can go faster," he said. "But I would have to get out of the car to do so and run alongside."

"Please!"

"*Señorita,* I am going faster than I can. *Rosinante* has not gone this fast in weeks."

"What is your name?" she asked.

"I am called Pipo," he said. "At your orders, *señorita.*"

"Pipo, I am in a desperate hurry!"

A black Mercedes with little Spanish and Moroccan flags on the front fenders cut in front of the *gasógeno*. The taxi driver cursed the man in sheik's clothes who lounged in the back seat.

"May he have boils on his feet and be made to deliver the mail!" he said. "I ask you, why this tribute from everyone to this man Franco, who killed so many? Who killed my son and my nephew? And now they honor him because, why? Because the war is almost over and he kept Spain neutral? Hah! Everyone knows he is a bandit and helped that monster Hitler in every way. Don't you agree, *señorita?*"

"Take a right here," she said. "Shorter."

"America, a great country, *señorita,*" said Pipo. "I assume you are American?"

"Pipo, faster, faster!" said Mia. "Very urgent!"

They reached the river, turned right on Paseo de las Delicias, and stopped at the handsome two-story building that was the American Consulate. In front, the maroon sedan with the gold seal on its side idled, and the chauffeur held open the back door as Consul Tottle, natty in a tuxedo, hurried out of the Consulate's grilled gate. His wife, in white and a little gold-and-diamond tiara, was already in the back seat of the car.

"Wait!"

Mia leapt out of the taxi and thrust herself between the Consul and his car.

"Mr. Tottle, please help!" she cried. "It's him – he's getting away!"

"Who?"

"I don't want to say his name – but you know who!"

Startled, Tottle stopped. "And you are–?"

"Mia Alvarez, and–"

"Ah, yes. German."

"I'm Wilson's friend, Mr. Tottle, and–"

"And where is Wilson?" said the Consul. "Supposed to go to this reception with us."

"He's with my friend Gilly from the English Consulate! They're hostages!"

Tottle hesitated.

"Hostages?"

"They're headed down the river on a boat called the *Cayetana*."

"Dear lady, what in hell am I supposed to do about it?"

"Can't you call up your armed forces?"

"Armed forces? What are you talking about? Spain is a neutral country!"

"Caleb!" A voice, slightly accented, came from inside the car. "Come, pet, we are *very* late."

"Dearest, we have a problem," he called to her.

Mia tried to blurt out the rest of the story in broken sentences, but Tottle cut her off.

"Dear lady, I will telephone Madrid, I promise! As soon as I get back."

"Too late," said Mia, grabbing his arm. "Do it now – every minute counts!"

"Caleb!" his wife called. "We will be late!"

"My dear," said Tottle, disengaging Mia's hand, "I'm

very sorry, but this is truly an important function."

"Don't you care that your Vice Consul's life may be in danger?"

"Madam, of course I care, care very much. But I have my duties!" He turned to get into the car, but Mia got there before him, leaning into the back seat.

"Help me, Frau Tottle," she said in German to the handsome, aloof woman. *"Sie seind eine Deutche* – you're a good German. Don't you want to see justice done to this Nazi monster?"

"I am an American citizen, my dear," she said in English, "The Allied authorities will take care of it." She leaned out of the car and commanded: "Caleb! Do get in!"

The Consul, avoiding looking at Mia, stepped into the back seat, the chauffeur closed the door, and the car started off.

Mia stared after the car. Thank you very much, you cold bitch, Mrs. Ingrid Tottle, she thought. What had the German Consul said her maiden name was? Farben?

Farben!

I.G. Farben, Industries.

The great maker of Hitler's munitions.

And gasses, Wilson had told her. Those super-efficient lethal gasses for the showers in the concentration camps, which she had tried to believe didn't exist, which were unthinkable.

No wonder Mrs. Tottle was in no hurry to apprehend a bigwig Nazi; she probably was a Nazi also, if only in her heart, maybe even an old friend of his, the murderer. Mia shoved her hand into the pocket of her dress, felt the reassurance of the little pistol, and turned to the waiting taxi driver.

"Pipo," she said, "stoke up *Rosinante*. We're going to Cadiz!"

13

After watching *Cayetana* glide out into the middle of the river, Moriarity felt a frightening emotion such as he hadn't felt in years: Desire for revenge burned inside his chest as never before. He was almost sure that he'd seen a top Nazi, a man like the one who'd destroyed his wife so long ago in Berlin. That it might not be the very same man did not matter.

What was that Nazi – could it be Martin Bormann as rumored – doing in Spain? Fleeing the Russians, the Americans, and the British, obviously. How had Wilson come to find himself on that boat with him and how had he got mixed up with a Nazi? Must be that German girl, the pretty von Wurmbrandt woman.

That was the only explanation.

Was Wilson perhaps a hostage?

What to do? Calling Madrid, the O.S.S., would take too much time, and informing Consul Tottle would be an exercise in futility. No, he would just have to catch up with the boat himself, at a bridge probably, and, if possible, somehow confront the man. And then what? Who knew? One step at a time.

Moriarity glanced down at his gas gauge – low, very low. He hated to waste the time, but he couldn't risk running out of gas. He pulled into the Querencia bar next to the spindly single gasoline pump that read "C.A.M.P.S.A." He punched the horn twice and then twice more.

Facundo Montero appeared. "All right, all right," he grumbled, wiping his hands on his apron. "Who needs the filling up so badly – you or your car?"

"Both," said Moriarity, handing the old *matador* some precious rationing stamps. "But I've no time for a drink."

"There is a first time for everything, I see," said Facundo unlocking, the pump and putting the nozzle in the tank. "A modest miracle that will rank along with the loaves and the fishes."

When it was done, Moriarity shoved some crumpled *pesetas* into Facundo's hand and started the car.

"Where does the river end?" he asked.

"What river?"

"This river, you bloody idiot!"

"The noble Guadalquivir," said the unflappable Facundo, "empties into the Atlantic at San Lúcar de

Barrameda, around the corner from Cadiz."

"So what road do I take?"

"Since there's only one road," said Facundo, "the choices are somewhat limited." He pointed down. "*Compadre*, I can't help noticing you've a very bad rear tire."

"I suppose you just happen to have a new and very expensive one to sell me."

"At your service always, *señor*. But friendship more than greed motivates me to tell you that tire is more bald than *El Gallo*, and—"

"Facundo," Moriarity said abruptly, "do you have a pistol?"

The old man's eyes narrowed. "A pistol, *compadre*?"

"A pistol, a rifle," Moriarity said impatiently. "A shotgun?"

Facundo shook his head. "I used only a sword, *amigo*, although many times in the arena I longed for a pistol. You may borrow my sword."

"Too big," said Moriarity. "Anything else?"

Facundo went back into the bar. He came out in a few moments with a six-inch dagger, a wooden handle at the end of a lethal-looking heart-shaped blade.

"*La puntilla*," the old *torero* said. He slid the weapon into a leather sheath and handed it through the car window. "It has given many a bull the *coup de grâce*. Please bring it back."

"*Gracias*, Facundo," Moriarity said, putting the knife in the breast pocket of his jacket.

"What do you intend to do with it, may I ask?"

"Give the *coup de grâce*," said Moriarity, "to a man."

Facundo's old eyes widened. "I have never killed a man."

"Neither have I," said Moriarity grimly.

"Let me change that tire," said Facundo. "It is precarious."

"No time," said Moriarity. "Tomorrow."

He shoved the car in gear and drove away. After speeding across the Triana bridge, he screeched to the right and drove along the river, headed south.

Now he was on Paseo de las Delicias, and he'd have to pass the American Consulate; he hoped it would not coincide with Tottle and his wife's leaving for General Franco's function about this time. It would be tough explaining any of this to the Consul, who was none too swift to begin with.

Moriarity was relieved to see the Consulate car was not out in front; they'd already gone. He felt bad for Colette. She would wonder where the hell he was, and she'd bought a new dress for the reception and was excited about it. But he had no time to stop and explain things to her, and she would only be upset if she knew the cause of his agitation.

Beyond the fashionable suburbs of Heliopolis, he braked at the crossroads. One sign pointed to Antequera and Málaga, the other pointed to the right: Jerez de la Frontera, Cadiz, and San Lúcar de Barrameda.

Moriarity swung to the right.

In a short time, he came to two police motorcycles parked across the road and a pole across two sawhorses, blocking any passageway. These blockades were, of course, the reason the fugitive German had chosen the river route.

No problem. Moriarity showed his diplomatic passport to the curt policeman, they lowered the pole, and he continued on his way. War or no war, this was standard procedure under Franco's paranoid regime.

Moriarity's Ford would not do better than fifty-five miles per hour, but five minutes past the blockade he caught up with an old taxi, chugging along with a *gasógeno* apparatus on the back. As he came alongside, he glanced at the occupant, wondering what a taxi was doing so far from the city. Moriarity caught a glimpse of a woman in black in the back seat, honked his horn, waved at the old driver, and sped past.

Ten minutes later, on the open road, nothing but wheat fields on either side and far from the nearest village, Moriarity felt a bump, then heard what sounded like a rifle shot. There was another jolt, a flapping sound, and the car wobbled over to the shoulder of the road with an exploded rear tire.

Moriarity cursed and sprang from the car. Since he never drove outside the city, he had no need of a spare. There was a pump in the back of the car, but the tire was in tatters. He ran his fingers through his graying hair. Except for the distant silhouette of a farmer haying in the field, he was alone, with the road to Cadiz stretching emptily before him. He banged his fist on the hood in frustration.

There was nothing to be done except to walk a long way back to the roadblock and ask the police for help. But what would one tell them one was doing out here?

"Sure and I'll be tellin' ye, officers, oi'm out here doin' a little promotin' for the good ol' Sinn Fein! Have a wee drink, fellahs, oi'm always out here in the country at night with no one about, and I welcome ye!"

Then he saw a car coming down the road. It was the old taxi he had passed. He waved to flag it down, and it drew alongside. The back door opened.

Mia von Wurmbrandt de Alvarez said: "I think you are a friend of Wilson's."

14

The police boat's siren wailed once, and the *Cayetana* throttled down to a stop.

"Do not any ideas get," the German hissed to Wilson and Gilly. "We are a happy group traveling together. No tricks, only yes and no answers, no details!"

The two Guardia Civil officers jumped from their boat onto the deck of the *Cayetana,* their automatic rifles at waist level, pointed toward the passengers.

"*Señores,*" said one of the officers politely but sternly, "*y señoras!*"

He was very handsome, movie-star handsome, Rudolph Valentino. He marched to where Klaus, the big German Vice Consul, was sitting.

They're looking for the other German, not Klaus, Wilson thought; let's *see the wily bastard get out of this one.* He glanced at the German, who sat rigidly, his face impassive, his left hand in the pocket of his raincoat, trying to look nonchalant. Gilly nudged Wilson in anticipation.

"Passport, please," said the handsome *guardia.*

The German Vice Consul looked down at the barrel of the rifle pointed at his chest. He hesitated, then reached in the side pocket of his jacket and drew out a bright blue booklet. The *guardia* saw the German diplomatic seal on the passport, didn't bother to examine it, and then bypassed the little man with the briefcase. The two *guardias* walked slowly by Moses Byrd and nodded to him; they weren't looking for a black man. The handsome *guardia* strutted past Miss Gold, who was still sound asleep sitting up, and stood in front of the German.

"Nationality?" he demanded.

The German stood up slowly. "American," he said, looking hard into the officer's eyes, but smiling.

"Passport," the *guardia* said.

"Certainly," said the German with elaborate courtesy, the bigger charming smile emerging, the killer smile.

He drew the green booklet from his pocket with his right hand, his left still on his hidden pistol.

Wilson felt his heart pound as the Spaniard riffled through the pages of the passport.

"*Vino?*" asked the *guardia.*

"I beg your pardon?"

"Wine business?"

"Yes," said the German, still smiling that smile.

"*Jerez?*" said the *guardia*.

The German's smile faded somewhat. "*Jerez?*"

"*Sí, Jerez de la Frontera?*"

"Oh, yes, of course," said the German.

The policeman made a drinking motion, with his thumb toward his mouth.

"You like our *Jerez?*"

He doesn't know what the hell you're talking about, Wilson thought.

The German finally caught on. "Ah, yes," he said genially. "We Americans call what you call *Jerez* after the city where it is made – er, that is, grown – developed, distilled, you know, we Americans call sherry."

"And you like our famous drink, *señor?*"

"Like it?" exclaimed the German, "I sell it all over America! I drink it every day myself."

Sure, oh sure, Wilson thought, *along with der schnapps und eating der schnitzel. Why doesn't the cop examine the passport?*

As though on cue, the *guardia* opened the passport again, looked at the photo, then at the German's face, then back at the photo.

"*Amigo,* have a good trip," he said with a smile. He snapped the passport closed, handed it back, and moved away.

Wilson felt like grabbing the policeman and shouting *can't you see it's been doctored? Can't you hear how he says ah-may-ree-kah? Are you tone deaf?* But now the two men were standing in front of Sidney Phillips.

"You are–?" said one of the *guardias.*

The bullfighter stood up.

"Sidney Phillips, *Matador de Toros,*" said the bullfighter. "I am American, at your service, and I…"

He never finished the sentence. Valentino had grabbed him by the sleeve of his jacket, deftly yanked him around, and at the same time his partner snapped a pair of handcuffs on the astonished man's wrists.

"Hey, what the hell are you mugs doing?" Phillips roared. "Don't you realize who I am?"

"*Si, señor,*" said Valentino, contemptuously, "we realize who you are."

He glanced at the youth, who remained seated, looking disinterested and as bored as though he were in church. "And what you are."

"What the hell you driving at?" said Phillips, struggling against the handcuffs. "This kid and I are just taking an outing down to Cadiz for the day. Nothing more, nothing less." Phillips looked around the cabin. "I am a full *Matador de Toros.* I am a killer of bulls, for God's sake!"

"And perhaps," said the *guardia* solemnly, "a killer of young boys."

"*Chíngate!*" Phillips spat out.

Valentino smiled at the obscenity. Both officers positioned themselves on either side of Phillips, then pushed him out of the cabin, across the deck and boosted him up over the side and onto the police boat's deck. The plump boy followed meekly and was helped aboard the other boat by the *guardias*.

"I'll get the American ambassador on the phone!" Phillips was yelling. "You guys will be out on your asses so quick you won't know what hit you!" Then he repeated the threat in Spanish. The police boat's motor spat twice and rumbled into life.

"They're leaving," whispered Gilly. "I don't believe it. They're leaving! We're sunk! Can't we stop them?"

With what, pray tell? thought Wilson. And the worst of it was the loss of the only real ally they'd had. Phillips was strong; he and Wilson might have cooked something up against the two Germans. Now what?

"We must stop them!"

"How?" Wilson answered lamely.

As the police boat pulled away from the *Cayetana,* he could hear Phillips roaring foul imprecations in Spanish at the police, the Guardia Civil, General Franco, and the Spanish nation as a whole.

The German stood and crossed the deck to speak in a low voice to the German Vice Consul. He was facing away from Wilson. The other passengers were watching the departing police boat and listening to Phillips's rantings.

"Mr. Tripp," Gilly whispered.

"Wilson, please."

"Wilson, listen. Important! I must tell you that it was no coincidence I showed up at Mia's when *he* was there. My boss is British Intelligence. Our man in Madrid spotted *him*," she nodded toward the German, "at the train station. Yesterday. His fancy shoes gave him away. Our Sevilla agent followed him from the station to Mia's house, called my boss. Then Mia called, very much in distress, and I went over. Oh God, poor Mia. Maybe better for the sick child, I suppose, but Mia, Mia! Obviously, she was shot when she was phoning me, probably *because* she was phoning me."

"Are you armed?" Wilson asked.

"No, I'm not an agent. Do you know who *he* is?"

"Suspicions."

"So do we. Got to stop this boat. Can you do it?"

"Maybe."

"Try! Oh God, do try!"

Wilson squeezed Gilly's knee and whispered, "Here goes."

He slipped into the passageway leading to the engine room. The captain was ten feet ahead at the wheel, but he had his back to Wilson and was engaged in steering the *Cayetana* through the bumpy wake of the police boat. He glanced around him as casually as he could. The girl was nowhere to be seen. *Here goes.*

Wilson took the knife from his pocket. He looked around once more and then opened it. He leaned down deep into the workings of the engine. Chunking, noisy, greasy. He knew nothing of motors of any kind, but he knew that little hunk of yellow rubber was it.

It took only two stabbing, sawing slashes to sever the hose between the fuel filter and the carburetor. He straightened up. No one was looking his way. He folded the knife and started to put it into his pocket. No, he might – probably would – be frisked. Reluctantly, he strolled to the rail. He glanced around and then casually dropped the knife overboard. The captain had not turned, had not seen him. He walked slowly back down the passageway and slid onto the bench next to Gilly. She was smart. She said nothing at first.

The German still had his back to him, standing casually, pretending to talk idly to Klaus; fellow travelers getting acquainted, nothing more, to any observer.

Klaus had seen him return from up forward. Wilson saw that Klaus kept glancing over at him now.

"Yes?" Gilly asked under her breath.

"Yes," Wilson said.

"Good fellow," she said. "Splendid fellow."

They sat in silence, waiting and listening as the boat chugged its way down the river. Wilson's fast heartbeat was loud in his ears and unnaturally in tune with the engine. They were in the center of Las Marismas now, the swampy area that made up one of the great bird sanctuaries of Europe, endless grassy wetlands on both sides of the river. They could see flocks of big white birds flying over the herds of black fighting bulls on the islands in the swampy ground.

Then they heard the first cough of the motor. A few moments later came another, and then three chuff-chuffs, and abruptly the vibration of the engine ceased altogether. The boat kept moving with the current of the river but no longer under power.

"Tana!"

They heard the captain bellow. He yelled for the girl to come to the wheel house to steer while he looked at the engine. In a few moments, he stuck his head in the main cabin. "We go to shore," he growled.

"The matter?" the German said, striding across the cabin to him. "The matter is?"

"Engine," said the captain, and turned to go to his wheel house.

"Fix it," the German barked after him. "A bonus if you fix it quickly."

Looking at his watch, the German slumped down onto the bench next to Wilson.

Sweat, you bastard, Wilson thought. *Your submarine is going to leave without you.*

Using the current adroitly, the captain veered the boat toward the right bank. He headed toward a small, tree-shaded cove and at the last moment swerved the *Cayetana* upstream. The prow then slid into the wedge of water and speared into the earth of the bank with a jolt. The captain and the girl scrambled off the deck with lines in their hands, which they made fast around the trunks of two olive trees. Then the captain came back into the cabin.

"*Señores y señoras,*" he growled in his hoarse voice. "We are here for a while. There is a *cortijo* nearby, the *cortijo* of Don Joaquín Del Monte, who owns these lands. I will go there and telephone back to Triana for the part."

Miss Gold had finally awakened. "Huh! The matter here? Have a ship, a ship, gotta catch it."

"I, too," said the German Vice Consul. "A ship to catch."

"*Señores,* you will all catch your ships," said the captain. "We merely need a small part for the engine which has somehow broken. Meanwhile, Tana will give you something to eat on board."

"What part has broken?" demanded the German.

"Fuel filter hose," said the captain. "To the carburetor."

"I will look," said the German. "Show me. About motors I know."

He went forward and peered down the open hatch into the engine. "You have tape – you can tape that hose together."

"No, *señor.* It would not hold." The captain shook his head. "Too much pressure, chance of fire. Besides, I have no tape."

"How did this happen?"

"Things happen, *señor,*" the captain said. "On boats, they happen."

The German stared down at the engine again. "It does not seem broken to me," he said, frowning. "It looks cut."

"Cut, broken," the captain shrugged. "Who cares? It does not matter, the boat will not go without a new one."

They went back into the cabin. The captain then walked to the prow, saying, "Passengers, I shall return shortly."

"Wait," the German ordered. "I must get to a telephone. I go with you."

"I also," said Klaus, striding across the cabin.

The captain shrugged. "If you like to walk."

"Suddenly Miss Gold called out: *"Auf Wiedersehen."*

Automatically the German replied: *"Auf Wiedersehen."*
Then quickly he added, "Goodbye, *madame.*"

He turned to Wilson and then to Gilly. His mouth widened into what was his most cordial smile.

"I'm sure you two feel like a stroll before dinner."

Wilson looked him in the eyes.

"Actually, we'd prefer to stay on board."

"Actually," the German hissed, "you are most anxious to take a stroll!"

He gave Wilson a sharp prod with the pistol barrel. Wilson rose slowly. Then Gilly stood up. The three followed the captain off the prow of the boat. Klaus and the little man brought up the rear as they climbed the path from the river. At the top of the bank, across the vast wetlands, the group could see two white buildings shining in the twilight, less than a mile away. They were the only visible dwellings on the vast horizon.

"There you see the *cortijo* of the great Joaquín Del Monte," said Nacho. Wilson knew the name, of course, one of the greatest bullfighters of all times. He'd read about him in books, had seen scratchy and silent black-and-white films of him; under different circumstances, he would have been excited to meet the legend. Maybe help lay ahead in this ranch house. At least being off that damned boat for the time being was good. And though it looked as though they were in the middle of nowhere,

Wilson could see the spindly telephone poles with their single wire marching across the eerie landscape to the white dwelling. Few private homes had telephones; they were in luck.

A pair of eagles shrieked overhead. Beyond the bulls, Wilson could see herds of fallow deer, a few bucks, but mostly does with their freckled fawns. In the grass beside the path, a fat red fox, unafraid of the humans, loped after a rabbit as though more interested in exercise than food. A griffon vulture, its bald head shining in the twilight, crouched nearby, its hooked beak slashing into the entrails of a fallow fawn. Flocks of kestrels socialized in the oak trees, whose trunks were white-washed with guano.

Soon the path became a wide road amid the swampy land. The Vice Consul came alongside the German and in a lowered voice spoke to him in German as they walked ahead of Gilly. A herd of black bulls was feeding far off to their right.

"Some of Don Joaquín's brave ones," said the captain. "But do not be afraid. When in a herd and at that distance, no charge. Only when one bull separated he becomes dangerous, he kill anything that move."

Even though they were a hundred yards away, Wilson felt a grab in his stomach, knowing first-hand what those needle-sharp horns could do and how fast the great beasts could run. One of the animals lifted its head and looked curiously at the people. Like its fellows, it had never encountered dismounted humans before. The bull took a step forward and snorted once. It wagged its great horns and pawed the ground. It was huge and old: the seed bull.

"Do not make sudden movement," said the captain. He stopped and the others pulled up behind him. He turned to Klaus. "It is you he is looking at, *señor.* Not at you, *señor,* but at this."

The big German had his raincoat slung around his shoulders, its sleeves flapping when he walked.

"The motion attracts him." The captain carefully took the coat from the man's back, folded it up, and tucked it under his arm. "Now we go, slowly. Very, very slowly."

The bull watched them warily for a few moments. But then, feeling unthreatened, it dropped its head and went back to eating.

Gilly hung back a few paces from the others and motioned for Wilson to do the same. "Been eavesdropping," she whispered while pretending to look over at the bulls. "Be careful…"

"Of what?"

"Of him – Klaus."

"You understand German?"

"Had a German governess for five years," she said. "Klaus just told his cohort that he thought it was you, that you had wrecked the engine. Klaus is dangerous. He thinks you are in the way."

"That's nice," said Wilson.

"Wilson," she said. "I think he means to kill you."

He couldn't answer.

They trudged on. Wilson made out a group engaged in

some activity on the grassy field at the side of the main house. As they drew closer, he saw six people. They were standing around an open grave.

15

"I've got it!" exclaimed Miss Gold. "Wow, have I got it!"
She slapped the sleeping Moses Byrd on the knee triumphantly. "I know who he is!"

"Who – who is?" he replied drowsily. "Who *he,* may I
ask?"

Only three of them were left on the boat now: Moses,
Miss Gold, and the girl, Tana, whom they could hear
bustling in the galley. Miss Gold glanced toward the
sound of pots and pans and slid over on the bench, close
to Moses.

"The man!" she whispered, pointing in the direction
the others had gone.

"You mean Mister Boyd?"

"His name is *not* Boyd."

"You don't say," said Moses, yawning. "May one ask what it really is?"

She glanced warily again at the galley, then hissed: "Bormann!"

Moses nodded and echoed. "Bormann." Then he sat up straight.

"Yes," she said vehemently. "The Nazi. Martin Bormann."

"Aw, come on," said Moses with a grin. "Come *on*, Miss Gold."

She shook him. "Martin Bormann. I think that's who he is!"

Moses took off his old homburg and ran his hand over his white hair. "Miss Gold, I sure don't mean no disrespect, but I have observed that you have consumed a couple of sherries and–"

"Bullshit," said Miss Gold. "I am almost positive that he's the monster who killed millions of helpless people."

"Man, oh, man," said Moses. "How do you come by such special knowledge?"

"I've seen pictures of Bormann," she said.

"But last night they said on the radio that Bormann died, same time as Hitler," said Moses. "The Russkies done killed him in Berlin."

"Bullshit," said Miss Gold. "He's right here in Spain, right here with us, escaping hanging, on his way to South America probably."

"How come you be so sure it's him? He claims he's

American."

"As American as apple strudel!" she snorted. "In English he's got a German accent. And when I tricked him into saying *Auf Wiedersehen* just now, it was pure Hamburgese. I've read Bormann is from Halberstadt, near Hamburg. I know that accent, my parents grew up there! People from Halberstadt tend to say *Oaf Wiedersehen,* whereas others pronounce it *Owf Wiedersehen.*"

"Miss Gold, you trying to convince me you can tell where folks are from just by hearing them say a few words?"

"Hobby all my life."

"Okay, so where do I come from?" Moses challenged.

"Virginia, maybe West Virginia," she said slowly. "I'll go with Virginia."

The widening of his eyes told her she'd hit home. "I'll take a chance, go further, and say the southern part of the state. How about Roanoke?"

Moses didn't speak for a moment. Then, "Wow, you is impressive, Miss Gold. Okay, so that guy is Martin Bormann, so now what?"

"We inform the authorities, that's what!"

"Uh, just which authorities did you have in mind, Miss Gold? I don't see no authorities around here."

"That young man, Wilson, the Vice Consul?"

"What can he do?"

"Arrest Bormann, that's what he can do!"

Moses gave her a gold-toothed smile. "Without a gun?"

Miss Gold pondered this. "They said they were going

to Don Joaquín Del Monte's *finca* to telephone. Don Joaquín has always been pro-American." She stood up. "He will help me. Are you coming?"

Moses didn't move. "I don't want to get involved with no German Nazi," he mumbled uncomfortably. "Had enough trouble with the Spanish ones."

"Then, Mister Byrd, I shall go alone."

"You can't do that, Miss Gold!"

"They killed my beloved sister and her husband," she said softly. "This is one Nazi who isn't going to get away."

Still clutching her manuscript box, she walked toward the prow of the ship.

"Miss Gold, you can't go up there alone," said Moses.

"Hell I can't," she said.

"There are bulls out there in the fields. I can see 'em. And it's getting dark. Don't go, Miss Gold!"

But now she had jumped from the boat's deck to the bank. She landed on all fours but quickly picked herself and her box up and lurched up the hill.

Moses sat watching her small figure disappear into the gathering darkness. Then he sighed. "One never knows, do one."

He humped himself to his feet with the aid of his silver-headed cane. "Wait up, Miss Gold!"

16

As Wilson and the others drew closer to the group around the grave, they could hear a young priest intoning: "And so we commit Thy servant, Diego Mateo, into Thy hands, oh Lord."

The captain stopped, removed his beret, and motioned for the others to halt as the burial group began to murmur the Lord's Prayer.

"Nuestro Padre, que estaís en los cielos…"

When they finished the prayer, the ceremony was over. The priest motioned to two men of the group to pick up their shovels and fill in the grave.

From photos, Wilson recognized the owner, the great old *matador* Joaquín Del Monte. It wasn't that he looked so old – but how small he seemed! He was dressed in the gray bolero jacket and the flat *cordobés* hat of the Andaluz rancher.

The captain approached Del Monte, who was shaking the priest's hand and giving him some money. The priest, a hook-nosed young man with a fringe of blond hair around a bald pate, looked remarkably like the griffon vulture they had just seen eating carrion.

"Don Joaquín," said the captain, "I am Nacho Perez of the *Cayetana*. The engine has trouble. I would like to use your telephone, if I might. These people are my passengers. They are American, or something foreign."

"My house is your h-house," said Del Monte. He made a sweeping gesture that included the big main house, the separate dwelling for servants, the little semi-sunken bull-ring for testing the animals, and the corrals. "We have just buried my old foreman, a good man." He hesitated for a brief moment. Then he added, as though obliged to say more: "But he was misguided. Our war, our t-terrible civil war, changed people's v-values. This person, not a bad fellow, was caught helping Germans, Nazis in fact, to get to South America via Cadiz. I, myself, had no part in his death. Other than this flaw, he was a good m-man." He hesitated, then added, "But a bred-in-the-bone Falangista."

Wilson didn't know what to say. Or rather he knew exactly what to say to Don Joaquín, *but when?*

Wilson had forgotten that Hemingway had written that this great *matador* had a lifelong stammer. The man had a wonderfully ugly face, piercing eyes like obsidian olives, a raptor's nose, and a jutting wolf jaw. His black hair had no hint of gray despite his almost sixty years. One writer had said he had "the look of eagles," and it was true. He went to each of the passengers in turn and shook hands. First to the little man with the briefcase. Then to Klaus he said, "My, *señor,* you are taller than the Giralda!"

To Gilly he said, in almost perfect English, "You are lovely, my dear," and kissed her hand.

When he came to the German, he looked hard into his face.

"Do I not know you, *señor?*"

"I have not had that pleasure, sir. I am Seymour Boyd from America."

Del Monte kept looking at him.

Strange, if it was Bormann, Wilson thought, how no one seemed to recognize him for sure. Hitler's right-hand man; he might look vaguely familiar to people, but the number-two Nazi in the world did not have a face that had been overly publicized and was instantly recognizable.

"America?" said Del Monte.

"Yes," said the German.

"A fine country," said Del Monte.

"Yes," said the German. "Fine."

Del Monte turned to Wilson. "I must come to your office next week, Mister Vice Consul. Now that the war is as good as over, I must buy some new farm machinery through you. We Spaniards can make guitars and sherry and sonnets, but that is all. We must even send our oranges to England to be made into marmalade, which they then sell back to us. Imagine! And now, speaking of that, come into the house for some refreshment."

The group, including the priest, followed Del Monte the fifty yards into the house, the workers going into the kitchen.

Wilson wondered how he could get Del Monte alone, tell him the situation. Then Del Monte could inform the Consulate, alert the Embassy in Madrid, alert Gibraltar, alert *somebody* to help. He was not pro-German, like so many wealthy Spaniards; he would not want this Nazi to escape.

As they entered the house, Del Monte gestured to the dining room, where Wilson could see food and wine laid out for the wake.

"Please, my friends, help yourselves to whatever you wish. It is not just an idle Spanish platitude – *mi casa es su casa.*"

The living room was simple; one would not immediately know it was the domicile of a bullfighter. Instead of the customary mounted bull's head over the large fireplace, a red stag glared down. A small Velázquez canvas of a peasant hung on one wall, a Goya drawing of a dwarf on another. On yet another wall hung a red-handled *estoque*, the bullfighting sword, in an engraved silver scabbard. There were bookcases everywhere, for while Del Monte had had only three years of grammar school for an education, he was well known as an intellectual, the friend of artists and writers, international and Spanish. A grand piano with a shawl on it was covered with photos. There was Del Monte with King Alfonso, Del Monte with Douglas Fairbanks, Marlene Dietrich, Charlie Chaplin, Garcia Lorca, Hemingway, Ortega y Gasset, Lindbergh.

The only other taurine touch in the room was a full-length portrait by Zuloaga of the young Joaquín Del Monte, striding from the ring, jaw jutting defiantly, a stream of blood running down one leg, a bull lying dead in the background.

Looking at the portrait, Wilson said: "May one ask, Don Joaquín, how many times were you gored?"

Del Monte smiled. "Quite a few, *señor*, quite a few."

"Ten times?" Wilson ventured.

"Oh more, many m-more."

"Twenty?"

"More."

"Fifty?"

"F-fifty is a good number," said Del Monte. "Let us say f-fifty. Yes, I like the number f-fifty."

He glanced down at Wilson's legs. "And speaking of gorings, I believe I heard that you have known one in Mexico."

Wilson nodded. "My knee."

"The *matador* El Tato," said Del Monte, "lost more than that. He lost an entire l-leg in the early days. Went on fighting with a wooden one."

Wilson smiled. "I can assure you I have no such ambitions, Don Joaquín."

"Well, it must be confessed that after that El Tato had little s-success." Del Monte gestured at the dining table.

"*Señor,* please h-help yourself to some food, some wine."

Wilson saw that the German was several feet away – far enough – feigning interest in the Velázquez.

"Don Joaquín," Wilson began in a low voice, "it's urgent that–"

At that moment, the captain approached. "The telephone, *señor,* if one may ask?"

"Certainly," said Del Monte. "Follow me. The bathroom is there also."

He walked away into the bedroom, followed by the captain. When Del Monte emerged, the German went in to wait his turn at the phone. Wilson started to speak to Del Monte again. Abruptly, the German Vice Consul came between them, the silent little man trotting by his side like a growth attached to his hip.

"Haffing a luffly trip?" said Klaus in his high voice. His skin was pitted, with a texture like the shell of a peanut. Wilson looked back at him coldly.

Klaus went on when Wilson didn't answer: "How strange that the boat should haff stop just after you came from near the engine. Does it not strike you strange, Herr Vice Consul?"

"Marine motors are *so* undependable," Wilson said, adding with elaborate respect, "Herr Vice Consul."

"Klaus!" It was the little man with the briefcase, pointing at a photo on the piano. "Look. Charlie Chaplin!"

It was the only thing Wilson had heard him say. Could this really be the famous scientist, Hans Roediger?

A bent old woman servant shuffled in, offering a tray of glasses filled with sherry and brandy. Wilson took one, as did the German.

"You may think the war is over, American," said Klaus, throwing down the brandy in one motion. "It is not. For you it is not. You will see."

The bedroom door opened and the captain came out.

"The *taller* is closed, does not answer the telephone. I must go back to Triana myself for the part. But how?"

"I have a car and a chauffeur." Then Del Monte apologized, "But no petrol and no coupons until Monday."

The priest put down his sherry. "You may come with me," he said. "My Fiat is old but dependable."

Klaus turned to him with fierce eagerness. "You have a car, Padre? Can you not take us to Cadiz?"

"*Señor,* from here the road goes only north on this side of the river," said the priest. "Besides, my little car holds only two people."

"Damn," said Klaus. "And how long will you be?"

The captain downed his brandy and said: "A few hours, with luck."

He and the priest thanked Del Monte for his hospitality and departed.

The German came out of the bedroom, and Wilson saw he was smiling. He exchanged a brief glance with Klaus and a barely perceptible nod. Something had gone right with his telephone call. Had the present delay been reported to someone who would get word to the ship or submarine that the German was counting on? He appeared smug and confident.

Wilson looked at Gilly. She, too, had seen the exchanged glances. She gave a defeated shrug, along with a what-do-we-do-now expression.

Del Monte came up to the German. "So, you made your telephone call. B-business surely. You Americans are all b-business. Relax, *señor,* have a good time."

The telephone!

"*Perdóneme,* Don Joaquín," said Wilson. "The bathroom?"

The old *matador* gestured to the bedroom. Without glancing at the German, Wilson walked quickly to there and closed the door. An austere white room. A gilt headboard at the end of a big bed. A crucifix on the wall. A photo of a pretty woman – wife? mistress? daughter? And a telephone on the bedside table!

Wilson went to it and snatched it up. He clicked it twice. And again. Dead. He looked down. Of course. The cord had been yanked from its socket after the German made his call.

Wilson went to the bathroom, then walked back out to the living room. Del Monte was sipping his sherry and saying to the German: "*Señor,* I have been to your fine Estados Unidos several times on my way to Mexico and South America, and I must say that…"

The white-haired servant shuffled up to them like an aged tortoise.

"Excuse me, Don Joaquín," she mumbled. "But there is a woman at the front door."

Del Monte frowned.

"A woman? Out here?"

"A woman and a man," she said. "A moor."

He strode to the door and opened it. There stood Miss Gold in her black dress, clutching her box with the manuscript in it. It was dark outside, and Moses behind her was almost invisible.

"Don Joaquín, I am sorry to intrude," she said, excited and breathless from the walk. "Important, very important. I've come from the boat and–"

"*Señora*," said Del Monte with alarm. "You came across those fields in the dark? Those b-bulls are very dangerous and unpredictable."

"Had to come," she gasped. She lurched, from fatigue and sherry, into the room. "That man," she leveled a trembling finger at the German. "I know who that man is! It finally came to me!"

The German stared back at her, a slight tight smile on his face.

"Monster!" the little woman said, stumbling toward him, brandishing her thick manuscript box out in front of her like a weapon. "Arrest him!"

Klaus stepped in front of her. "Be quiet, you stupid old woman!"

"Fuck off, buster," she said, pushing past him. "He's the criminal, you're just a second-rate punk!"

"*Madame,* you have made a mistake about me," the German said, with a little bow. "You are taken in wine, excuse my saying that."

"Kill him!" Miss Gold whispered. "He's the Nazi, Martin Bormann, the murderer of millions!"

"*Madame*, I am Seymour Boyd of Wilton, Connect-it-cut."

"Yeah, sure," she said, "and I am Clara Bow from Malibu Beach! You see, he can't even pronounce the state he says he's from! You killed my family, you bastard!"

She lunged toward him.

"*Verdammt noch mal!*" the German ducked and said quietly. "*Goddamn* you, woman."

Klaus drew his pistol.

"*Nein*, Klaus!" shouted the German.

17

"*Nein!*" commanded the German again. "Klaus, *nein!* Don't shoot!"

But the pistol fired once, and Miss Gold was slammed back against the wall. She slid slowly down, the manuscript box still clutched to her chest.

Gilly gave a cry and ran to the fallen woman.

"Miss Gold!" Wilson knelt by her, as did Moses.

The old woman whimpered, her eyes glazed, "Nazi, Nazi…"

Gilly lifted the thick box up gently. There was no blood on her shirt, no blood anywhere.

"Miss Gold, I am a nurse," said Gilly. "Where are you wounded?"

The old woman, breathing shallowly, didn't answer. She seemed in shock. And then Wilson saw it, saw the black hole at the center of the manuscript box. He turned it over. There was no exit hole. It was almost comical; the hundreds of pages had stopped the bullet.

"Miss Gold," said Wilson, smiling. "You are all right."

"Thank the Lord," said Moses Byrd.

The old woman didn't seem to understand that Columbus had saved her.

Del Monte strode over and commanded, "Take this poor woman to the bedroom." He whirled on the German and Klaus. "And you, sirs, leave my house immediately!"

But the German had his own pistol out and was pointing it at the old *matador.* "Regrettably, *señor*," he said, "this must be our house for the next few hours. Do not be worried. We trust you will indulge us, and then no one will be harmed. I apologize for Klaus."

Del Monte snorted. "Now I can see you are exactly what this p-poor woman called you!"

"We are citizens of the Third Reich," said the German proudly. "We are good citizens, good men, patriots. In great ideals we believe. And we are now on a mission of enormous importance!"

Del Monte gave a dry laugh. "I think you are Nazi b-beasts and not as worth living as the good animals in my f-fields." He turned away in disgust.

Gilly and Wilson helped Miss Gold to her feet. She stood there shakily for a moment, then pointed to the box on the floor. Moses picked it up and handed it to her. She hugged it to her chest, and, like a somnambulist, let herself be led to the bedroom by Gilly and Moses.

Del Monte was looking at the Germans with contempt. "I assume you are on your way to South America, like the other c-cowards of your tribe."

"Be careful," Klaus warned. "Be very careful, sir, I have a temper."

Del Monte went on as though Klaus hadn't spoken. "You know, I admire General Franco for many things – after all, he saved Spain from the C-Communists. But never did I approve of his unholy alliance with your l-late unlamented madman of a leader."

Klaus shoved his pistol in front of the Spaniard's face. "Be careful with your mouth, old man! He was our *Führer!*"

"Why be careful?" asked Del Monte simply. "Since you shoot old and unarmed women, you surely intend to kill us all before you are through h-here. Why should I not have the brief pleasure of insulting you?"

"Now hear me, *señor,*" said the German in a placating tone. "I apologize for Klaus, but who talks of killing? We are stuck here for a few hours, against the will of every person. When the captain arrives with the boat part, poof, we are gone and no one the worse."

He saw Del Monte's gaze flicker to the sword in its sheath on the wall.

"And we are not bulls, *señor.* Do not play the hero – do not think like Quijote," he pronounced it *kee-shotey,* "do not make us kill you. Now, *señor,* sit down in that comfortable chair and rest until the captain returns."

Del Monte glowered, but there was nothing to be done except to do as ordered. He turned and, with an angry sigh, sank into the big leather chair.

Moses and Gilly came back into the living room.

"She's fine," said Gilly. "Sleeping like a baby." She glared at Klaus, who looked away. "I'm sure you are pleased."

The German stood in the middle of the room. "Now pay attention, all of you. We will surely be back on the boat at dawn. But now we must get through this night without excitements. You, *schwartze*–"

He pointed at Moses, sitting quietly on the couch. "You stay right where you are, understood?"

Moses nodded. The German looked at Gilly and Wilson. "You two I do not trust. Klaus has found a very nice place for you two. Show them their suite, Klaus."

Klaus grinned and motioned with his pistol to follow him. They went from the living room through the dining area. At the end of the room, a door stood open. By the single dim bulb that hung from the ceiling of the little basement, Wilson could see wooden barrels.

"In!" commanded Klaus, with a slash of his pistol.

When Wilson hesitated, the German grabbed him by the shoulder roughly and wrestled him through the door and down four steps. Gilly stumbled in after him; had he not caught her, she would have fallen to the earthen floor. The heavy door slammed shut, and they heard what sounded like a metal bar drop across to lock it.

They looked around them. The dank basement room

was no wider than ten feet, but it appeared to be about twenty feet long. It was filled with huge barrels of wine. Sherry, *manzanilla* and *amontillado,* Wilson guessed from the heady, rich smell. A small passageway separated the two stacks of barrels, and Wilson used it to walk the length of the room.

There was no other door, no windows, and only two high air vents, too small for a human to crawl through. They were there for the night.

The barrels, on saw horses, were all stacked on their sides, and when he came back to the front of the room, he saw that Gilly was sitting up on one with her back against another. She had undone the bun, and now her black hair with that intriguing white stripe was down to her shoulders. How could she look so comfortable and unruffled?

"Well, Stanley, another fine mess you've got me into," she said with a charming little smile.

What a cool customer, Wilson thought; he had to match it. He heaved himself up next to her on the big barrel.

"You like Laurel and Hardy?"

"All your American films. They helped get us Brits through the war, I'll tell you. As much as your Liberty ships. I must have seen *Casablanca* twenty times, in between air raids."

Wilson said in his best Bogart, "I came to Casablanca for the waters."

"But, my dear Rick," she countered, "there *are* no waters in Casablanca."

Wilson pantomimed taking a drag on a cigarette.

"I was misinformed."

"Not bad," she said. "But the trick to doing Bogart is to immobilize your upper lip. Freeze it, then everyone sounds like Bogart." She lowered her voice. "You played it for her, Sam, you can play it for me."

Wilson knew they were both straining to keep their spirits up, and he was grateful.

He smiled. "You were in show business?"

"Script girl at the Ealing Studios when the war started."

"But you said you were a nurse."

"Nurse's aide. I said I was a nurse just to give that poor old woman confidence in me."

"That bastard, Klaus," Wilson said.

Mention of Miss Gold brought both of them back to their situation, and they fell silent. Then she said: "Submarine, I heard Slyboots tell Goliath a little while ago. The *Marlin* it's called. He knows exactly where it's supposed to surface tomorrow."

"No Cadiz?"

"No Cadiz."

"That's not good. If we pulled into Cadiz, we might have a chance of alerting someone, with all the other boats and ships around."

Wilson saw two silver testing cups by a smaller sherry barrel, across from where they were sitting.

"*Madame,*" he said. "May I interest you in a small, shall we say, aperitif?"

"According to W.C. Fields," she said, "when you're in a jam, nothing better than a little *espiritu fermentae.*"

"Well, we're in a jam, all right."

He went to the barrel, held the cups under the spigot, filled them, and handed one to Gilly. "Here's to you," he said.

She dipped her head. "My father had a wonderful ribald toast. Something about *may you live as long as you want to, and want to as long as you live,* but mercifully I've forgotten it."

They drank.

"The Spaniards have a wry toast," he said. "*Salud, pesetas y amor sin suegra* – health, money, and love without a mother-in-law."

They drank to that.

"How'd you end up here in Spain?" he asked.

"Goes with Noël."

"What?"

"Coward," she said. "I'm a coward. My last week in London, three months ago, I was in the operating room, helping with a guy left over from the Battle of the Bulge. Younger than you. Brave kid, brave as hell. They were trying to save one mangled arm. He'd lost the other plus both legs at the hip. They tried, but they couldn't save the arm. I went to the loo, threw up, quit, went down to the Consular Corps and said I'm yours. They sent me to sunny, peaceful Sevilla, and here I am."

"Some peace," he said.

"Indeed."

"What I don't understand," Wilson said abruptly, "is why they haven't just killed us."

"It's certainly not out of the kindness or whatever they have in place of where real humans have hearts."

"What, then?" he said, knowing what then.

"Hostages. We are bargaining chips, somewhere way down the line in their plans."

"And then–"

"And then dispose of us. And Don Joaquín, I'm worried about him. He has horses in the barn. As soon as they leave, he could ride for a telephone or help to intercept them."

"I'm sure they've thought of that." Then he said, "You're pretty casual about all this."

She smiled and tapped her chest. "You should see it from in here."

"You're a good actress then."

She sang softly and well. "You must remember this, a kiss is still a kiss…"

"You planned on going into that, acting?"

"Not at all. I wanted – still want – to be an architect. And you?"

"I love painting, but as a career? I don't know about that, either."

"My dad was a painter. Well, an architect first, then a Sunday painter. He was painting, it was Sunday in Cricklewood, when the bomb fell and killed both my parents. In the garden at tea time."

"How awful."

"I don't know. One might say, what a way to go. No old age, no cancer, no cataracts, no loss of love. Dad was such a great old rowdy bugger. People said he wore life like a loose garment, and it was true. Mom was sweet, a good mother, sort of a self-proclaimed invalid and hypochondriac. But I've still got my grandmother. She's so smashing. She looks like your George Washington. We call her Wonky."

"I'd like to meet Wonky."

"You'd like her. She's the best fisherman who ever cast a fly on the Test River."

"Now I know I'd like her."

"You fly-fish?"

"Is there another way?"

She took off her glasses.

She really was a good-looking woman. Very good looking. Beautiful English white-and-rose skin, almost transparent, incredibly green eyes. Full breasts under the cashmere sweater.

"This is the place in the movie," he ventured hesitantly, "where the boss says, 'Why Miss Kelly, without your glasses you're beautiful.'"

She gave a little laugh. "Thank you. I'll keep 'em off from now on."

"Are you married?"

She shook her head and looked down. "Fiancé. Dunkirk. Drowned."

"I am sorry."

She sighed. "Long time ago. And no one ever died from a broken heart. I even have a hard time remembering exactly what he looked like. But he was a smashing chap."

"No new loves?"

"Never dated since. I'm afraid of love. I guess I'm known as an ice maiden, the Nun of Cricklewood."

"As bad as that?"

"Maybe these glasses are part of my defense. I'm like the woman in the P.G. Wodehouse story." She gave a little laugh and put on a professorial voice. "Known in native bearer and half-caste trader circles as She On Whom It Is Unsafe to Try Any Oompus-Boompus."

She grew serious again. "It's just that everyone is so damned *dead*. So damned dead forever in this stupid war. So many wrecked lives and stupid deaths all because of" – she gestured upward at the door – "because of *them* and their kind. God, I would like to see those two fry in hell!"

"Maybe we will. We're going to get out of this mess."

"You think so?" she asked, a sudden tremor in her voice. She wasn't as tough as she tried to appear.

He eased his arm around her shoulder slowly. It wasn't cold, but he said, "It's cold," to justify his action. She didn't resist. She leaned into him.

Was it only their terrible situation that made him feel so close to her – the heightened emotions they were all experiencing? How had he been so mistaken about her at first?

"Gilly?" He wasn't sure what he wanted to say.

She turned her face up to him. He kissed her forehead, her cheek, then her lips. Then again, deeper.

"So nice," she murmured, pulling her head away for a moment to look at him. "Such a long time."

She kissed him hard and moved his hand to her breast. They were both breathing hard when the door suddenly slammed open. Wilson saw two figures silhouetted at the top of the stairs and heard Klaus snarl: *"Verdamt schwartze!"*

The next moment, a body was flung down the four stairs and the door was banged shut. Moses Byrd landed hard on the earthen floor.

Wilson jumped off the barrel and knelt by him.

"Moses!" He helped the man to his feet.

"I get the distinct impression," Moses mumbled unsteadily, "that the gentleman doesn't care for me."

"Are you all right?" Gilly asked anxiously.

Moses got up shakily and sagged against a barrel.

"Well, I got two black eyes," He said with a weak chuckle. "But you might say I had them before that bozo hit me."

Gilly filled a cup full of sherry and gave it to him.

"What did you do to anger him?"

Moses drank and said: "Well, I was sittin' there thinkin' and thinkin' about what we could do about our predicament, and I come up with this oh-so-brilliant idea. You know that pretty sword of Mister Del Monte's that's hangin' on the wall? Well, I wait till the big old Kraut has his eyes closed, sleepin', and I slither over to the wall, and I have that beautiful piece of steel inched half out of the scabbard, and I'm fixin' to stick him good, and all of a sudden he wakes up and is across that room and is on me like a tiger. Whacked the hell outta me with that pistol, and I found that mighty rude, I don't mind tellin' you."

"We'll get him tomorrow," Wilson said. "We'll get both of them."

"And don't forget the midget with the briefcase," said Moses.

"Him, too," said Wilson.

"You *really* think we'll be all right?" Gilly asked, as though he had some fantastic plan he hadn't shared with them.

Suddenly Wilson realized they looked to him as The Leader. But he was no leader.

"Yes," he said with as much conviction as he could muster. "I know it."

And then he thought, like Jake Barnes: *Isn't it pretty to think so?*

18

It was not yet dark when the ancient taxi finally chugged up to the bridge of María Sagrada across the lower Guadalquivir. At this time of year, it stayed light in Andalucia until nine at night, and the length of the span was clearly visible even without the lighted lanterns spaced at twenty-foot intervals.

In the long, agonizingly slow ride in the taxi, Moriarity and Mia had soon discovered that they had a common enemy and a common purpose. But how to accomplish it?

"The bridge is very low," he had said. "And the river is high now. I think I'll be able to drop onto the boat's deck fairly easily."

"But what about me?" she exclaimed. "I am the one who must kill him! I must, for my daughter's sake!"

"How?" he'd asked. "How in the world can you kill him?"

"With this!"

She snatched the .25 caliber Krüpp pistol from the pocket of her dress.

"Holy fuck," he exclaimed and then added: "Excuse me, ma'am."

She handed the pistol to him.

"Hallelujah," he breathed. "Oh, yes!"

"It was my husband's."

"What a good girl," he said, as he caressed the Krüpp. "A lovely little German piece. *Madame,* we are in luck!"

Then he slid back the chamber. And his face fell.

"What?" she said. "You don't like it?"

"It's a lovely gun in all respects," he said. "Except one."

She looked at him, not understanding.

"You have bullets?"

"Oh, God! I assumed – it never occurred to me to look. I don't know anything about guns. I have no bullets!"

"Never mind," he said trying to keep the disappointment out of his voice. He put the pistol in his pocket.

"I have a knife," he said, taking out the *puntilla* dagger, wicked-looking even in its little scabbard.

"But what about me? I want to make him pay for what he did!"

He shook his head. "You told me he thinks you're dead. He must not see you, my dear, or the jig will be up.

You drop me off at the bridge, then the very best thing you can do is you and" – he gestured at the driver – "head for Gibraltar and alert the British Navy. They'll love your news. There's almost sure to be a sub waiting off Cadiz for the bastard. The British'll blow it out of the water. It will be the happiest day of my life when I see that happen."

He took a card from his wallet and wrote on it. "Here," he said. "If you can't get through to the Gibraltar brass, and let me tell you they're impossible to contact, then call this number in Madrid. It's O.S.S. Ask for Aline. If you have to, ask for her by her code name, Tiger. This is her home phone. She'll get things hopping. They don't call her Tiger for nothing."

They arrived at the bridge and stopped. Pipo climbed out to stoke *Rosinante's* heater with coal. Moriarity took out his silver flask and offered it to Mia.

"Good Irish whiskey," he said.

"*Gött,* I could use it," she said, tilting it up. She swallowed a little, gagged, and passed it back to him.

He drained it and slid the flask back into his pocket. He opened the door.

"Good luck," she said. "Kill him dead, dead, dead!"

He nodded. "I've a pretty good reason myself for wanting to wish him, well, unalive, as it were."

He reached out and put his hand tenderly on her shoulder, then abruptly blurted out in German: "I, too, knew a beautiful Germany once."

He kissed her on the cheek, got out of the car, and strode off as *Rosinante* chugged away.

The bridge was low slung, narrow, and well lit. Nominally a drawbridge, it was seldom raised these days, as only the steamship *Marqués de Comillas* and a few tankers came up the river, irregularly, to Sevilla. Off to the left, shimmering white in the far distance, ten miles away, lay the legendary port of Cadiz, where the freighters and other large ships anchored. Water on three sides, almost an island, protruding into the Atlantic toward the Americas. And there was San Lúcar de Barrameda. Columbus sailed from that port on his third voyage. Magellan, too, set sail there to go around the world in 1519. And here he was, Francis Xavier Moriarity, waiting for the grubby tub *La Cayetana* to heave into sight.

He walked to the center of the bridge and stood under a light. The brighter the better. He wanted to be seen by the Germans on the boat, and the sooner the better.

But where *was* the damned boat? *Rosinante,* slow as it was, traveled faster than the *Cayetana,* but the vessel should have arrived by now.

He sat down, legs dangling. He took the useless pistol out of his pocket and turned it over in his hands. God, what he'd give for just one lousy cartridge! He started to throw it into the river. But then he thought of a use for it, a very good use for it, and put it back into his pocket.

He looked up the quiet river. He made out a lone fisherman on the bank, the only sign of life in the twilight, and he waited. He rehearsed his lines; it had been some time since he'd spoken German, a language he'd once known well.

Another drink would go well about now, a whole bowl of Mister Bushmill's whiskey. It might be a long night. And he must not get himself killed.

Who would take care of Colette?

19

"Pipo," Mia instructed as they drove away from the bridge.
"We go now to Gibraltar!"

The old taxi driver shook his head. "I'm sorry, *señorita,* I cannot. First, I am a Spaniard. Gibraltar, by all rights, belongs to Spain and always has, but the wretched British who stole the rock from us in 1704 won't let ordinary Spaniards go there. They will let me go as far as Algeciras and no farther."

"I could walk across the border."

"Ah, but the second problem, *señorita,* is *Rosinante.* She is almost out of coal, and she would not make it. Gibraltar is a long way from here, not as the crow flies but as the *Rosinante* puffs."

"Then take me to a telephone."

Pipo gestured at the empty fields on both sides of the taxi. "Even if there were houses or farms, there are few of those *aparatos* in this part of the world. In cities, yes. Not here."

"There must be a telephone nearby."

"In Jerez de la Frontera," said Pipo. "There are many *aparatos*."

"Can we make Jerez?"

Pipo shrugged. "We can try, *señorita*. It is twenty long kilometers away." He patted the dash. "I hope *Rosinante* will not fail us."

It was dark an hour later when the old taxi finally chugged into the town of Jerez de la Frontera, sherry capital of Spain. They drove past wineries and at last down the pretty, tree-lined main street, finally coming to a coughing stop in front of a brightly lit entrance. A sign hung over the doorway, a painting of a swan with *Hotel Los Cisnes* written underneath.

"*Gracias,* Pipo," Mia said, giving a handful of pesetas to him. "Go feed yourself and *Rosinante*."

She hurried into the well-appointed lobby and spoke to the concierge. He pointed to a booth. "Just give the *centralita* the number you need, *señorita*."

She went in, closed the door, and picked up the phone.

But then she put it down. Who would she call in Gibraltar?

Obviously, some British or American admiral or commander or captain in charge, but who would believe her crazy story?

She took out the card Moriarity had given her. She gave the Madrid number to the operator. An old woman's voice answered. *"Diga?"*

"May I speak to Aline, please," Mia said.

"One moment."

A younger voice came on the phone. "Yes?"

"Aline?" Mia said.

"Who is this?"

"My name doesn't matter, but you've got to do something quickly."

"Are you sure you have the right number?"

"Are you – Tiger?"

There was a silence. "I don't know what you mean."

"The man from the American Consulate told me to call you. You are Aline, aren't you?"

"My name is Miss Gardner," was the chilly answer. "I don't know who you are, but we should not be talking on the phone like this."

"It's an emergency. I'm calling from Jerez and–"

"Come see me tomorrow in the Embassy. This phone is not secure. I am at home."

"Tomorrow is too late! This is terribly important to your country!"

"Then it definitely should not be discussed on the phone. I am going to hang up now."

But before she could, Mia blurted out, "He is here from Germany!"

The voice said quietly, *"Who* is here?"

"You know who I mean, I'm sure. The Nazi. He's in Spain, right now, in a boat going down the Guadalquivir. The boat is called the *Cayetana*."

There was skepticism in the other's voice. "You've seen Mister Nazi?"

"Yes, oh, yes indeed, I have! And he's on his way to rendezvous with a submarine tomorrow, I'm sure!"

"*Madame,* I don't mean to be rude, but we get many strange calls. Just today, there have been two reported sightings of Adolf Hitler in the park here in Madrid."

"You must believe me," said Mia frantically. "I'm not crazy."

"How do you know he is who you say he is?"

"Because he is my godfather," Mia said. "And he is a murderer."

"Your godfather," she said, unconvinced.

"And Wilson Tripp from your Sevilla Consulate is with him. He's been taken as a hostage."

"Your godfather has taken the Vice Consul as a hostage," she said flatly. "Just how did you get this number?"

"A man – he told me."

"What man?"

"The man on the road – I don't know his name!"

"You-don't-know-his-name," she repeated slowly. "The-man-on-the-road."

Mia was exasperated. "You don't believe me," she said. "But it is true, and he must be stopped! You must stop him!"

"We'll look into the matter," the woman said, but her tone did not assure Mia. "And what is your name?"

"Mia von Wurmbrandt, and I live in Sevilla, where–"

"Did you say," the voice on the other end suddenly had changed its tone, "Wurmbrandt?"

"Yes," she said.

"Are you by any chance married?"

"He's with the Blue Division in Russia. But that has nothing to do with–"

"Would his name be Alvarez? Lieutenant Luis Alvarez?"

"How do you know my husband's name?"

It was now a different-sounding voice on the line.

"My dear, my office has been trying to reach you for two days. Didn't Stryker, the German Vice Consul, inform you?"

"Inform me?" Mia's voice quavered. "Inform me of what? He's dead, isn't he? He's dead!"

"On the contrary, your husband is in Madrid. He's been wounded, but he's very much alive and anxious to see you."

A great sob burst from Mia.

"Thank you," she whispered. "Thank you."

"We're glad to give you the good news, of course, but that isn't why we were looking for you. Your husband told us of your connection with *that* person. I don't want to say his name on the phone. We've been following his trail, and a bloody trail it is. We thought he might try to reach you."

Mia could barely respond. "He did, oh God, he did."

"I'll get on this matter right now with Gibraltar. Meanwhile, bring yourself here to Madrid as soon as you can. Your husband is in the Clínica de la Merced. I'll take you to him."

"Danke, danke," was all Mia could say before hanging up.

20

The sound of a motorcycle woke Wilson up the next morning. It took him a moment to realize where he was, half-sitting, half-lying on a barrel, in a cellar somewhere in the wilds of the Marismas of southern Spain. Gilly was asleep against his shoulder, but she awoke with a start when he moved his arm from around her.

"What time is it?" she said groggily.

He glanced at his watch. "About six."

Moses was asleep, stretched out on two barrels.

Wilson stood up stiffly and went to one of the air vents. By standing on a barrel he could see out: A motorcycle sputtered in the courtyard, a young man at the controls, the captain of the *Cayetana* in the sidecar, triumphantly hefting a package. The German, smiling, was talking to him. When the captain got out of the side-car, the motorcycle drove off. The captain and the German disappeared from view.

The door to the wine room suddenly clanged open. Klaus stood there, pistol in hand.

"*Und* now, seekers of fun," he said cheerily, "we get ready to go to the excursion boat. Please to wake up the *schwartze*."

Somehow, his being cheery was more menacing than his usual ugly disposition.

The three climbed up the stairs, and Klaus prodded them into the living room. Del Monte was still glowering in his chair.

"Good morning," said Klaus, as though this were a normal day and a normal situation. Del Monte said nothing.

The German and the captain came into the house.

"*Guten morgen,*" the German said amiably. "After a good night's sleep, we are ready to resume our little journey. Soon we are all safe at our several destinations, *nicht wahr?*"

He looked around. "Where's Roediger?"

So it *was* the famous scientist!

The little man, still shackled to his heavy briefcase, appeared from the dining room.

Roediger! The Roediger!

"Ah. Here he is. We go now, professor."

The German said something to Klaus in German under his breath. Then he drew his pistol and gestured at

Moses and Gilly. "You two will come with me and the captain and the professor. Klaus, you take care of things here. You know," he hesitated only a moment, "*everything*." He jabbed Wilson in the stomach with the pistol. "Bring him with you."

As Gilly turned to go, she touched Wilson's hand and said quietly, "Be careful. He says he doesn't trust you."

"Thanks," he whispered. "We're even. I don't trust him either." He watched her, helpless, as she started toward the door.

"And Miss Gold?" asked Wilson as the German and the others started to leave. "What about her?"

"She is fine," said the German, turning. "We do not need her. She will stay here, with our friend Señor Del Monte."

The bedroom door was closed; maybe they'd killed her already, he thought. Gilly turned for a final look back at him as she went out the door. Did Klaus mean to shoot him now? He had his Lüger in his hand.

But Klaus came up to him, smiling, and said, "You be a good boy now, eh? No more fool-fool with the engine, *jah?*"

It was as though it was a big joke. But then suddenly the smile was gone. "I do not trust you, Yankee boy."

"I have to go to the bathroom," Wilson said. "Do you trust me enough for that?"

"Be quick about it."

Entering Del Monte's bedroom, Wilson found Miss Gold on the bed, curled up in a fetal position, her manuscript box beside her. She seemed dazed but was very much alive.

"You all right, Esmeralda?"

"Young man," she murmured, "how is it you know my name?"

"I saw your passport in the Consulate. But are you all right?"

"I am fine," she said. "Just old. But you must stop him, you must *kill* him!"

He didn't say anything, but hurried into the bathroom. He flushed the toilet so that Stryker wouldn't hear him open the cabinet over the basin. As he'd hoped, Don Joaquín still shaved with a straight razor. He folded the steel blade into its ivory handle and slipped it into his pocket; there was no time to put it in his leg brace.

"Miss Gold, I'll come back for you," he said. "We'll get you on a ship to America, I promise."

"Good luck," she whispered.

When he came out he said to Stryker, "Quick enough for you?"

Stryker said nothing. He began to frisk Wilson, slapping his chest and sides. The third slap, on his pants, produced a hard sound.

"Ah, hah, and vat do we haf here?" He reached into the pocket and yanked out the razor. "Cut, cut, cut!" he chided, as he opened the blade and pantomimed slitting Wilson's throat with it. Then he snapped the razor closed, slid it into his pocket, and without a word smashed Wilson hard across the face with the back of his hand.

Wilson fell back and tasted blood on his lips.

"Before we get to Cadiz," Klaus whispered, "you will pay for what you did to the boat. I will take great pleasure seeing to that, believe me."

Wilson said nothing, his fingers to his mouth.

"We go." Klaus started out the door. Suddenly Del Monte was out of his chair and confronting the German, looking up into the big man's eyes. "You will not get away, you know!"

"To whom you speak?" asked Klaus.

"To you, you shooter of old women!"

Klaus looked at him with a small and terrifying smile on his face. "Don't like you, old man! You are shutting up!"

"May God strike you dead," said Del Monte. "You and your other murderers."

"God?" said Klaus. "Today I am God." Raising his pistol, he struck Del Monte in the face, the butt of the Lüger slamming into the Spaniard's temple. Without a word the little man rocked backward, then slowly sagged to his knees. He stayed for a moment as though praying. Then he rolled over on his side, his hands twitching, unconscious. The blood from the small cut on his temple trickled out onto the black-and-white tiles.

"Oh, God!" said Wilson.

Horrified, he stared down at the *torero* lying in front of him. "Jesus, man! Why – did you have to do that?"

"I did not kill him. He will be all right," Klaus answered calmly. "I didn't like him. Besides, he has horsies, he could ride for help. Now will be too late when he comes to. He may ride horsey tomorrow, but not today. *Raus mit ein!* Unless you wish to join him." He gestured down at Del Monte. "Now we go with the others to the boat."

Wilson kept staring at Del Monte's crumpled body – this man who had successfully defied death for so many decades. But his servants would find him; with luck he would be all right.

"Go!" Klaus prodded him with the barrel of his Lüger. Wilson turned and started down the path. God, he'd never hated anyone so much, never felt so powerless.

Klaus slung his gabardine raincoat over one shoulder, like the day before. Seeing the coat, an idea – a crazy one – flashed through Wilson's head. *Too dangerous!* He dismissed it before it could really take hold. But for that brief moment, he'd felt comfort. *Maybe!*

The air was clear and warm now, the fields were still damp, the sun was up, and if Wilson hadn't just seen a man, a good man, almost killed in cold blood, it would have been a lovely morning. The various little animals scurried about in the grass, and overhead raptors circled, looking for them. A lynx eyed them from a distance. In the far field the herd of cows and young fighting bulls grazed calmly.

The idea came back with a rush. As they moved over a hillock, Wilson's heart suddenly pounded as though it wanted out of his chest: The huge seed bull was right where he'd been yesterday. He was grazing alone, not fifty yards from the path. The animal raised its great head, wagged its horns, and stared curiously at the men. Wilson stopped, and the animal went back to feeding.

Maybe I could do it, Wilson thought, trembling. *I really could do it now. I may get killed, but I've got to try.*

Klaus was just about three feet behind Wilson.

God, do I have the guts? He could remember all too well what a horn tearing through flesh felt like.

"Why are you stopping?" Klaus growled. "Go!"

Wilson spoke as calmly as he could. "Herr Vice Consul, I don't believe you quite understand. See? This is not your basic farm animal. This is a fighting bull, bred to go at motion and to kill whatever moves. Please, don't get us killed!"

He stepped toward the German, who brought the pistol up to point at Wilson's chest.

"No tricks, now," he warned.

"Remember what the captain said yesterday? About your raincoat?" Wilson spoke like a schoolteacher. "How the motion irritated the animal? To keep the bull from charging us, the captain took it from you. Remember?"

He stepped closer. "Let me demonstrate. May I?"

He reached out. He did it unthreateningly, and casually he pulled the raincoat off the German's shoulder.

"For example," said Wilson, adjusting the raincoat in both hands, "never, never do this!"

Suddenly he whirled away from Klaus, and with the garment held out in front of his body, he sprinted toward the animal.

"*Ah huh, toro!*" he shouted as he ran. "*Toro, ah hah.*"

"What are you doing, you crazy!" he heard the German yell behind him. "You crazy man, stop!"

The bull raised its head at the annoying, challenging voice and saw the cloth and the man running toward him.

"*Huh, toro!*" Wilson shouted.

Now the bull had lowered its huge head and charged at Wilson. Its great bulk covered the ground with astonishing speed, the speed of a racehorse, the dagger-sharp horns headed for the flapping raincoat that Wilson held out in front of his body. "*Huh, toro!*" Wilson slid to a stop. Crouched over and profiled to the bull, he shook the cape a last time to focus the animal's attention.

Just before the horns would have hit the raincoat, Wilson snatched the target away.

The bull's speed and momentum carried its bulk eight feet beyond Wilson, leaving it directly in front of the German.

"*Mein Gött!*" the man screamed, backing up in terror as the animal bore down upon him. The pistol went off wildly. One more high-pitched "*Mein Gött,*" and then the German's body was hit amidships, as though he'd been struck by a speeding Ferrari. There was the crack of bone, a terrible yell, and the man was flung into the air. When he came down, the bull's right horn was waiting to impale him through the stomach. Once again, he was hurled into the air.

Wilson had already dropped the raincoat and was running

down the path. He was fifty yards away before he stopped and turned to see the fearsome spectacle. Breathlessly, he watched in terrible fascination as the enraged animal tossed its bloody victim again and again, like a cat playing with a catnip toy. It was soon over.

"That's for you, Don Joaquín," he breathed. He was shaking.

Now what? He was free to go. He could go back to the house and try to fix the phone to get help, but the German and the boat would be long gone by the time anybody arrived. What would happen to Gilly? Moses was an old man, but Gilly had her whole life in front of her. It was a life Wilson had become very interested in.

He took a last look up the hill. By now, several of the other animals had joined the seed bull, and, incredibly, they formed a circle around the man's dead body; Wilson had heard they did that, a sort of wake, but he'd never seen it.

Retrieving Klaus's pistol was now out of the question. He turned and hurried down the path. When he came in sight of the *Cayetana* he saw the German coming up the path fast, pistol in hand. "I haf heard shooting," he said. "What happens? Where is Klaus?"

Wilson pointed back to the fields, shook his head, and said: "I warned him, but he wouldn't listen to me."

The German looked at him suspiciously. "What are you meaning?"

"The bull got him, poor devil."

"I don't believe you!"

"Go look for yourself."

The German strode up the path. Wilson waited, and he felt good. He felt very good. In a few moments, the German came back, tight of face, his mouth working angrily, and his eyes blazing. "Why you didn't help him?"

"I warned him," said Wilson. "I said, 'Hey, Klaus, look out!' I said it really loudly."

"You could have done something! Run for help at least."

Wilson looked at him, shrugged, and patted his leg. "I'm sorry, I don't run well, *mein herr*. I have a bad leg."

The German stared at him. Wilson stared back, wide-eyed.

"Come!" said the German. "The boat is repaired and waiting!"

Roediger, Moses, and Gilly were in the stern in the fantail of the *Cayetana*. Wilson saw Gilly's face light up when she saw him.

As he sat next to her, she whispered, "Thank God! I heard the shots! I was sure something awful had happened."

"It did," he said, and squeezed her arm. "But not to me."

He was breathing hard. *My God, I've just killed a man!*

"Klaus?"

He nodded. "He won't be joining us."

She took his hand. "What happened?"

As the Spanish girl cast off, the boat gave a rheumy cough, backed away from the bank, and churned out into the current.

"Tell me," Gilly said.

But the German came over and sat next to them. "I am watching you two," he said, "very carefully."

21

An hour later, as they approached the bridge of María Sagrada, Wilson was the first to spot him.

He'd gone forward to use the head, and when he came out he happened to glance at the bridge in the distance. There seemed to be a man in dark clothes standing there on the railing. Fascinated, Wilson glanced at the captain in the wheelhouse; Nacho appeared not to have seen the strange figure yet. As they came closer to the bridge, the thought came to Wilson – the man looked like Moriarity!

A little closer, and he was sure. The crazy Irishman in his shiny black rumpled suit and red tie was standing up there, waving his arms, a perfect target, a sitting duck. What in God's name was he doing?

The German was back at the stern. Now the captain,

too, had seen Moriarity, and he quickly left the wheel-house to alert the German. "I think he is also from the *Consulado Americano*," Nacho said.

In a moment, the German was by Wilson's side, his pistol drawn. He looked curious but not alarmed. Why should he be? A sitting duck on a bridge, waving his arms like a madman? Gilly came up beside Wilson. "Is that who I think it is?" she whispered.

Wilson glanced at the German and put a finger to his lips. The German moved to the front of the boat.

Now they were close enough to hear Moriarity's voice. He was shouting something; it sounded like German. He heard the word *freund*.

Wilson took Gilly by the arm and moved her away from the German.

"What's he saying?" he asked.

"He's saying he's a friend, don't shoot, let him come aboard."

"They're not going to fall for that!"

The German seemed more amused than worried; he could kill this madman at any time.

Moses Byrd came forward and, leaning on his cane, said: "What in hell is that man up to?"

"I have no idea," said Wilson.

Moriarity kept up the diatribe in German.

"What's he saying?" asked Wilson.

"He says he's Irish, a Sinn Feiner, always pro-German, wants to help, wants to go with him to South America."

"They're not dumb enough to believe him."

Moriarty kept pleading as the boat drew closer.

"He says he knew friends of the German in Berlin," she said. "He's naming them."

The German seemed to grow interested in this.

"Now Moriarty is saying Mia is alive and has gone for help!"

"Jesus!" Wilson exclaimed. "Mia's alive? Then why in hell is he telling the German this?"

"Talk English!" the German shouted. "I don't understand your accent! What are you saying?"

"Mia von Wurmbrandt has gone to the British for help, to arrest you!"

"You are lying."

"Who else besides us," shouted Moriarty, "knows she has a head wound?"

That did it.

They were almost to the bridge when the German turned around to the captain. "Stop the boat."

The captain brought the *Cayetana* around and held it steady against the current. When the German strode to the stern, Gilly and Wilson followed. They were directly under Moriarty now.

"How do you know I am on this boat?" said the German.

"Bucko there told me. He blabbed."

The German glared at Wilson before turning back to Moriarty. "You are from the American Consulate?"

"Sure and I am," Moriarty said. "And the poor dumb fookers there have been thinking all through the war that

I was with them! Me, an Irishman, pro-German and anti-British, like any good Irishman! Let me come aboard and I'll help you get away."

"How do I know you haven't been sent to kill me?"

"Watch me," said Moriarity. "But don't be shooting me now!"

He reached into his pocket. Holding it by the barrel, he slowly brought out the pistol.

"This foine gun," he said, "you see it's German, not American, eh? And here's what I'll be doing with it."

He flung it far from him. It glistened in the air as it spiraled down into the river with a splash.

Jesus God, Wilson thought, *he could have shot the German dead and saved us all! He's gone crazy! I thought he was just acting!*

The German looked where the gun had sunk.

"Come aboard," he commanded, but he did not put away his own pistol.

Moriarity worked his way down to the lower spar. He grabbed it with both hands, hung for a moment, then dropped the ten feet heavily to the deck.

He stood up, dusted off his knees, adjusted his tie, and extended his hand to the German.

"Frank Moriarity, *mein herr,*" he said pleasantly, "at your service. And I'll be going with you."

"You threw away a good pistol," said the German. "Why?"

"How the hell else was I going to convince you not to shoot me, some lunatic American?"

"We have not much time," said the German. "What is this about the woman, Mia?"

"I met her on the road," Moriarity continued, avoiding Wilson's gaze. "She said she was on her way to Gibraltar, going to alert the British. My guess is that there's a sub-chaser or two on their way here right now. Listen, you better make tracks, *mein herr.*"

The German looked off to the left, past Cadiz toward Gibraltar, as though he could already see warships steaming to thwart his plans.

"Make speed!" he ordered the captain and pointed off to the right, toward the wide-open Atlantic. "We have no time!"

As they went under the bridge, the German took out a piece of paper, and his thick eyebrows came together as he consulted it. Then he strode to the wheelhouse to show it to the captain. *Coordinates,* Wilson thought, *that he'd been given back there on the telephone.*

Wilson edged over to Moriarity. "Frank, Jesus, Frank, what the hell is going on here?"

Moriarity turned and started to move away, but Wilson caught him by the shoulder. "You're not really going with him, are you? Have you lost your marbles? What about Colette?"

Moriarity whirled.

"Well, what about Colette?" he said angrily and loudly as the German came out of the wheelhouse. "You didn't really believe that crap about the Nazis violating her, did you? You want to know the truth? I'll tell ya the truth!

It was one of your precious G.I. soldiers that did the dirty deed! So there you have it! Now you know, Wilson m'boy, you know what's truly inside me, been inside me all along. You can take the boy out of Ireland, lad, but you can't take Ireland out of the boy, so t'hell with your stars and stripes, I say!"

Stunned, Wilson backed away. "Oh, Frank, Frank," was all he could manage to say. He went back to the far end of the stern, slumping next to Gilly.

"He's blown his stack," he whispered. "That's all there is to it."

"Or else he's faking it," Gilly ventured.

"He didn't fake throwing that pistol away!"

"Yes, why didn't he shoot the bastard?"

The *Cayetana's* engines were throbbing hard. The vessel had left the indulgent Guadalquivir River waters now, and the sudden strong wind and choppy waves, the deep ultramarine blue and viridian green sea, told them, no doubt about it, that they were out of the tame river water and into the no-nonsense, aggressive Atlantic Ocean.

Directly across from them, Wilson could make out the vague outline of North Africa, fewer than fifty miles away across the strait.

Africa! Morocco! Tangier!

Always romantic names to Wilson, but not romantic now. Perhaps the German was planning to go there, Tangier, instead of meeting a ship or a submarine out here, so close to Spain.

It made sense; Wilson had visited Tahnhair, as the

Spaniards called it, last month on a courier mission. It was a wide-open, international zone, a magnet for every spy, refugee, fugitive, and sexual deviant. And Germans, lots of Germans, especially Nazi Germans. It would be logical for the German to head for friendly Tangier; a submarine was probably right this moment sitting in the Tangier harbor, refueling and waiting for–

"Hey!" Gilly nudged him hard. "What's that?" She pointed to the left. "Over there!"

He saw a white streak on the surface of the ocean, a white arrow coming from the direction of Cadiz or, more likely, Gibraltar and headed straight for them. A small craft, perhaps thirty-five or forty feet long, sleek, low-slung in the water, and incredibly fast. When it came closer, Wilson could see that there were three men aboard. Then he saw that the boat was equipped with a large, double-barreled machine gun mounted on a swivel on the prow. A British flag was painted on the side, half-submerged as the boat raced forward. One man was piloting the craft, another manned the gun on the prow, while an officer stood in the stern. The boat was small but looked as streamlined, efficient, and deadly as a torpedo.

Now it slowed, settling down in the water, as it slid near the *Cayetana*. From forty feet away, the officer in the open cockpit barked an order to the fat sailor at the wheel, picked up a bullhorn, and shouted: "Ahoy, *Cayetana*, kindly kill your engines and heave to."

The tall officer of the British boat was young, very young, and pink-cheeked. But he seemed strong and authoritative. The sailor standing on the prow, his hands gripping the two handles of the hefty machine gun, was stocky, swarthy, and much older. He appeared to be tough and seasoned, probably because of the jagged scar that zigzagged down one side of his face. All three men wore short-sleeved, immaculate white uniforms.

Maybe we're saved, Wilson thought. *Yes, we are saved!*

"Captain Pérez," the officer broadcast, "stop your engines. Now!"

Nacho throttled back, and the two vessels drifted closer to each other. "What means this?" he shouted. "I do nothing! Why you stop me?"

They were so close now the Englishman didn't need amplification.

"Captain, your vessel will follow ours to port!"

"Which port you talking?" said Nacho.

"Gibraltar."

"I Spanish," growled Nacho. "I follow to no British port."

The lieutenant didn't raise his voice. "Captain, I have my orders. Now you have yours."

"To hell with orders," said Nacho. "I not go!"

The lieutenant picked up the microphone dangling from a cord from the radio next to the wheel. He spoke a few words into it. He listened a moment, then said quietly: "Captain Pérez, I am authorized to fire upon your vessel if you do not follow me into Gibraltar immediately."

"My boat Spanish, I Spanish," yelled Nacho. "I not go!"

The German strode quickly to the rail. He looked over

at the English boat, rocking in the swells, not fifteen feet away. With a disarming smile, he said in a folksy voice:

"Hear, hear, young man, what is this all about?"

"Orders, sir."

"What kind of orders, may I ask?"

"Sir, I can't say, but I am to bring your vessel in at any cost."

"At any cost! Well. Interesting." The German seemed to ruminate. "I can't imagine why. May I ask, what is your name?"

"Lieutenant Bingham, sir."

"I am Seymour Boyd, and I am American," said the German. "Lieutenant, why would anyone want to take us to Gibraltar when we are all headed for Cadiz to catch our ship to New York? At this rate, you will make us miss our sailing to America."

"Sorry for the inconvenience, sir."

The German gestured toward the fantail of the *Cayetana*. "Do you realize, Lieutenant Bingham, that young man over there is the American Vice Consul at Sevilla?"

"Orders, sir. Captain, start your engines."

The German was now edging down the deck. "Lieutenant Bingham, sir, you realize, of course, that you will be in bad trouble for this stupid maneuver."

The Englishman ignored him and said to Nacho: "Captain, for the last time, engage your engines and prepare to follow my vessel."

The German was now opposite the sailor at the

machine gun.

"And what is your name, gunny?" The German said it with a friendly smile.

"My name is Winston Churchill," the man growled in a Cockney accent. "And oi was in the battle of Dunkirk and the battle of Jutland, and oi don't think for a fookin' minute that you're an American!"

The German's mouth widened.

"Oh, but I am," he said. "Would you care to see my passport?"

He reached into his pocket and drew out the green American passport. He threw it over across the water, and it slapped onto the deck at the gunner's feet. "See? American!"

Then it all happened so fast that Wilson could barely follow the action.

The gunner took one hand off the machine gun to reach down for the passport. The German yanked the gun out of his pocket. There was a crack from the pistol, and at the same time a short, ineffectual burst came from the machine gun, the bullets thudding into the side of the *Cayetana*. The gunner jerked once, then slumped unmoving over his weapon.

The German whirled and shot the lieutenant, who crumpled to the deck, head first, then pulled himself up to his feet. His white shirt was turning red, but he staggered forward, grabbed the microphone and spoke rapidly into it, just before the second bullet tore into his neck and knocked him to the deck.

The fat sailor dropped the wheel, held up his hands in front of him, as though to ward off a punch.

"Oh God, please," he managed to whimper before the German shot him twice in the chest.

The German turned and barked at Nacho: "Captain, full speed. Go!"

Expressionless, the German glanced down the boat at Gilly and Wilson as the engine rumbled to life, and the *Cayetana* drew away quickly from the drifting English cutter with its dead crew.

"Good shooting," said Moriarity dryly.

Wilson and Gilly sat in stunned silence. He tried to catch Moriarity's eye, but the man was sticking close to the German, obviously avoiding any contact with Wilson.

The water was becoming choppier, the swells bigger, and soon the British boat was almost out of sight. Wilson felt a tap on his shoulder; it was the tip of Moses' cane. Wilson looked up at him. Silently, Moses jabbed off to the right with his stick.

Far in the distance, in between the foam-topped swells, Wilson saw a dark green shape in the water. Moses pantomimed a diving motion with his hand and then glanced over at the German and Moriarity. They were talking and hadn't seen the vessel yet.

But Captain Nacho saw the apparition. He yelled. "To starboard, *mi general!*"

The German shaded his eyes with his hand and stared across the water. He grinned. "By God, yes! There she is, *Die Marlina!*" He gave a little hop of joy. "Right where she should be!"

"Hooray," said Moriarity. "Will they let me come aboard too?"

"Of course," said the German. "You will come with me, Frankie."

Frankie! Jesus wept, Wilson thought. *Frankie, yet.*

The *Cayetana* pitched through the increasingly heavy swells toward the huge green shape.

Wilson had never seen a submarine before. It looked much bigger than he had imagined, a monstrous green whale.

Soon Wilson could make out not only the conning tower, but the decks awash with foamy Atlantic swells. Three men were launching a small rubber raft with an outboard. One of the sailors got into it, started the motor, and headed across the hundred yards that separated the two vessels.

"*General!*" Nacho called out in alarm, pointing to the left.

The German's head swiveled. One could just make out a gray shape in the distance, the low gray shape of a British sub-chaser, class A-203, the latest model.

He snorted in derision. "We will be submerged and long gone by the time it gets here. We haf no problem."

Moriarity took a step forward. "*Mein herr,*" he said, almost whispering. "You have one problem. One very *big* problem."

"And what," said the German distractedly, looking back at the approaching rubber boat, "is that?"

"Me," said Moriarity.

Now the German was interested. He turned and laughed. "You?"

"Precisely," said Moriarity. "I want to tell you something."

"Yes?" said the German.

"I think you are a dirty rotten pig." Moriarity's left hand shot out and grabbed the German by the collar, yanking him forward. At the same time his right hand, with the *puntilla* dagger, stabbed out toward the man's heart.

Only by an instinctive jerk to the right did the German avoid taking the blade in the chest. As he turned, he deftly caught Moriarity's wrist in his big right hand, spun him around, and the pistol in his left fired once. Moriarity staggered back, clutching his shoulder. Before he fell, the knife clattered to the deck.

Wilson leapt from his seat and flung himself at the German's back, wrapping an arm around his throat and at the same time gripped the wrist that held the pistol as tightly as he could. The two men rocked back and forth.

"Goddamn you!" Wilson hissed as he tightened his hold on the German's throat, his fingers digging deep into the man's thick neck.

Gilly suddenly yelled: "Look out, Wilson!"

Roediger had crept up behind the two fighting men and, with surprising accuracy, he swung the heavy case attached to his wrist, catching Wilson on the side of the head. The world went black for a moment, and Wilson sagged to the deck. When his eyes cleared, he saw his little assailant standing over him, about to bash him again with the case. But Wilson wrapped his arms around the man's knees and lunged up. Staggering down the deck, he carried the yelping man to the stern of the boat and wrestled him up and over the side. Roediger dropped into the water with a final cry, and the case attached to his wrist dragged him under. He struggled to the surface briefly, choking and gasping, thrashing desperately with his free arm, but the weight of the briefcase pulled him under again until only the fingers of his right hand, opening and closing, were above water, and then they, too, disappeared and a black beret floated to the surface.

"Wilson" Gilly shouted. "Come quick – he's getting away!"

Wilson turned back to see the German climbing up on the gunwales and shouting orders to the sailor in the rubber boat sent from the submarine.

Wilson sprinted to the knife and snatched it off the deck, but he was too far away to even try to stop the German. He was going to escape, the rubber boat was almost alongside.

"Bormann!" Gilly yelled. Then, in German, she screamed: *"Ach wie güt das Niemen Weis, das ist Martin Bormann heis!"*

Astonished at the perfect German, and something nonsensical, coming from the English girl, the German hesitated for a second and turned his head. It was enough. In that moment, Wilson saw a sudden dark figure appear behind the German.

"Hey there, Mister Kraut!" a voice yelled. Moses, swinging his silver-headed cane like a baseball bat, clipped the German hard behind the knees.

The German stumbled back onto the deck and caught Moses' follow-up swat across his temple. He staggered up to his feet, blood running into his left eye and down his cheek. The pistol in his hand flashed and cracked twice.

Moses stopped. His cane fell, and he clawed at his chest. His mouth worked silently in disbelief, he stumbled back three fast steps across the deck and collapsed heavily.

As Wilson ran toward him, the German pointed the gun and pulled the trigger. There was a click, and another click, and he threw the pistol at Wilson. Wilson ducked and lunged at the man as the German crouched to jump over the side. Wilson yanked the German off the gunwale to the deck and stabbed at his twisting body.

"*Schuft!*" the German screamed as the blade slashed into his elbow, ripped up his biceps, blood spurting out. But Wilson couldn't hold the powerful German, who squirmed his way out of his arms, dodged another thrust by Wilson, and, clutching his arm and leaving a trail of blood, lurched across the deck. He dove over the side and spilled into the rubber boat. The German sailor hauled him upright as he gunned the motor.

"Damn!" Wilson impotently watched the rubber boat bucking through the swells, back to the submarine. Then he turned and knelt by Moses.

"Get me home," the big man gasped. "Please get me home." Then his mouth worked soundlessly, his eyes closed, and he died.

"Oh, God," Wilson whispered. "Oh, Moses, no!"

He stood for a moment, looking down at the old face, dignified even in death. Then he stood up and hurried over to where Moriarity lay gasping on the deck. Gilly was already beside him, with a blood-soaked rag on his shoulder. Wilson knelt down by him.

"How goes it, Frank?"

"I'm all right, bucko," he whispered. "You – you got a piece of him, did you?"

The brogue was totally absent from his voice.

"We got a piece of him, Frank, you and I."

"So now maybe that SOB will get gangrene," he said. "Maybe he'll die on that sub."

Wilson looked at Gilly questioningly.

"We've got to get him to a hospital." Gilly said.

"Listen, bucko," Moriarity said weakly, raising himself to one elbow. "Do I or do I not get the Oscar for my performance?"

There were tears in Wilson's eyes. "You get the Oscar and the Nobel and the gold Bung Finger and whatever other prizes there are for acting. You almost fooled me, you bum; hell, you did fool me. You were magnificent, in an awful way."

Moriarity lay back, a beatific smile on his face. "Tell Colette," he said, and closed his eyes.

"One thing, Frank," said Wilson, "something I don't

understand. Why didn't you just shoot the guy when you were on the bridge with the pistol?"

Moriarity managed a wheezy laugh and whispered, "No bloody bullets."

"Jesus, Frank, pistols are supposed to have bullets."

"Now you tell me, bucko."

"Is Mia really alive?"

He nodded. "She must have arranged for the sub-chaser from Gibraltar."

"Good girl," said Wilson.

Gilly said. "Let him rest till we get to shore."

Wilson strode to the wheelhouse. "Listen, you son of a bitch!"

The captain turned away from the wheel and looked at him, cowed by Wilson's anger.

"We've got a wounded man and a dead man on board – get this Goddamned boat to Cadiz quick!" And just in case Nacho didn't understand the English expletive, Wilson added a few Spanish equivalents: "*Canalla, sinvergüenza, malaje, granuja,*" and, for good measure, "son of the great whore – *hijo de la gran puta!*"

The Spanish girl, close to hysterics, was trying to cover Moses' body with a tarpaulin. Wilson helped her tuck it under the lifeless mass.

"Sorry as hell, Moses," he whispered. "But we'll get you home. You were great."

One never knows, do one.

When he looked back over where the submarine had been, there was nothing; it had slid beneath the waves on the beginning of its long trip to where – Argentina? But Gilly was tugging at his sleeve. "Look, Wilson, look!"

The sleek, fast sub-chaser was almost abreast of them, headed for where the sub had disappeared.

Wilson and Gilly cheered the Englishmen they saw on the decks and pointed toward the spot where the submarine had been. The men waved and gave the thumbs-up signal.

Gilly and Wilson watched the great ship slide past amazingly fast; it could possibly overtake the U-boat.

"Go, guys, go," Wilson yelled. They watched it disappear around a promontory. Not too far from Trafalgar, Wilson thought, where another British ship, Nelson's *Victory*, had won a pretty good battle a few decades ago.

He sat down wearily on a bench in the stern, and Gilly joined him.

"What was that you said to him in German that stopped him?"

"I just wanted to stall his jumping any way I could," she said. "So I said the first thing that came into my head, the stupid riddle that the dwarf Rumpelstiltskin says in the nursery rhyme, you know, about no one knowing his name. I learned it when I was six. He thought I was crazy, and it slowed him up for a moment – but not long enough."

"And good old Moses gave his life to try to stop him," said Wilson. "God, all these deaths in less than twenty-four hours."

"At least Mia's alive."

"Somehow."

"What do you suppose was in that little German's briefcase?"

"We may never know." After a moment, he said, "But neither will the Japanese."

They were silent awhile, listening to the throbbing of the boat and the waves slapping its hull. Then she said: "What are you going to do now? I mean, when we get ashore."

"Get some sleep. Tomorrow go out to take care of Miss Gold. See that the State Department sends Moses to Virginia. Visit Frank in the hospital. Then report to Consul Tottle. Know what he's going to say?"

"Recommend you for a medal, promote you to ambassador?"

"Sure. What he's really going to say is 'There you go again, Tripp. What makes you think that was really Bormann? Name a card, any card!'" It was a good imitation. "'Got any proof, Tripp, or is this just one of your cockeyed theories? If you think I'm going to tell people in the State Department that Bormann, or whoever it was, got away from us, you've got another think coming!' Then he's going to say, 'And besides, my wife went to school in Berlin with Marty Bormann, and she says he vas soch a loffly leetle boy, he vooden do none of dose naughty tings.'"

"And then what are you going to say?"

"I'm going to tell him to shove it and quit the dear old Consular Corps, and then I'm going over to pick you up and take you to the Alfonso Trece for dinner."

"I think I'd like that," Gilly said.

"And no oompus-boompus," he added. "Not necessarily, that is."

She gave a little laugh.

"Then on Monday – by Monday the war in Europe should be declared over, and I'm going to take you over to Málaga. I know the most romantic little place–"

"A dank wine cellar?" she asked.

"Oh, no, it's–"

Then they heard it, far off and under water. A great *oomph*. They looked at each other.

Right afterward, another *oomph*. "Depth charges," he murmured.

"God," Gilly said. "Maybe – do you suppose?"

They waited. Nothing more.

"Maybe they got him," Wilson whispered. "Just maybe they got that bastard."

There was a third *oomph*.

"*Olé!*" he said.

She took his hand. "*Olé!*" They looked at each other and smiled. She leaned forward to kiss him.

"Hey!" came a hoarse voice.

"I hate to interrupt you two," Moriarity was propped up on both elbows, and the brogue had come back to his voice, "but what does a man have to do to get a fookin' drink on this foine vessel?"

Last Boat to Cadiz was printed by Capra Press in October 2003. One hundred copies have been numbered and signed by Mr. Conrad.

Twenty-six copies in slipcases were also lettered and signed by the author and by Gayle Lynds.

About Capra Press

Capra Press was founded in 1969 by the late Noel Young.
Among its authors have been Henry Miller, Ross
Macdonald, Margaret Millar, Edward Abbey, Anais Nin,
Raymond Carver, Ray Bradbury, and Lawrence Durrell. It
is in this tradition that we present the new Capra: literary
and mystery fiction, lifestyle and city books. Contact us:
We welcome your comments.

815 De La Vina Street, Santa Barbara, CA 93101
805-892-2722; www.caprapress.com